Deemed 'the father of the scientific
**Austin Freeman** had a long and distir　　　　　　　, ...⌄. ⌐⌐a⌐t a⌐
a writer of detective fiction. He was born in London, the son of a
tailor who went on to train as a pharmacist. After graduating as a
surgeon at the Middlesex Hospital Medical College, Freeman
taught for a while and joined the colonial service, offering his skills
as an assistant surgeon along the Gold Coast of Africa. He became
embroiled in a diplomatic mission when a British expeditionary
party was sent to investigate the activities of the French. Through
his tact and formidable intelligence, a massacre was narrowly
avoided. His future was assured in the colonial service. However,
after becoming ill with blackwater fever, Freeman was sent back to
England to recover and finding his finances precarious, embarked
on a career as acting physician in Holloway Prison. In desperation,
he turned to writing and went on to dominate the world of
British detective fiction, taking pride in testing different criminal
techniques. So keen were his powers as a writer that part of one of
his best novels was written in a bomb shelter.

BY THE SAME AUTHOR
ALL PUBLISHED BY HOUSE OF STRATUS

# From a Surgeon's Diary

R Austin Freeman & John J Pitcairn

Introduction by Norman Donaldson

HOUSE OF
STRATUS

This edition published in 2001 by House of Stratus, an imprint of
Stratus Holdings plc, 24c Old Burlington Street, London, W1X 1RL, UK.

www.houseofstratus.com

Typeset, printed and bound by House of Stratus.

A catalogue record for this book is available from the British Library.

ISBN 0-7551-0360-2

# CONTENTS

# FROM A SURGEON'S DIARY

## Introduction by
## Norman Donaldson

This series of stories, which has never previously been reprinted in volume form, was originally published in *Cassell's Magazine* in six monthly issues beginning in December 1904. They were preceded in that periodical by the two *Romney Pringle* series, which have recently been published by Oswald Train. Before these words appear, the same publisher will also have issued Clifford Ashdown's adventure novel, *The Queen's Treasure*, which has never before appeared in print.

As in these other Ashdown stories, *From a Surgeon's Diary* echoes the experiences and special interests of both the writers who shared the pseudonym. R Austin Freeman, who went on to create the immortal Dr Thorndyke, was living, by the time these stories were written, at Gravesend on the Thames estuary, and John James Pitcairn was within cycling distance as medical officer at the Borstal establishment for young offenders near Rochester.★

The stories are narrated by young Dr Wilkinson, who, like Pitcairn, was a graduate of St Bartholemew's Hospital, and, like Freeman, was forced by lack of capital to become locum tenens to a series of established practitioners in various parts of southern England, acting on their behalf while they were sick or called away. This is, of course, the career followed by Christopher Jervis prior to his long partnership with Thorndyke. Jervis called it "the old trail, the long trail, the trail that is always new," and Thorndyke added grimly, "and leads nowhere." Pitcairn avoided it by becoming a prison medical officer. Freeman was less fortunate; opting for the colonial service, his experiences closely paralleled those of the burglarious Dr Ringmer in the present series who observed: "I took a ship out to Accra seven or eight years ago and was fool enough to go upcountry a bit. I thought I was tolerably proof, but I caught a dose of 'black water' and very nearly joined the majority."

Freeman's uncertain health for years after his discharge – without a pension – made even a career as a "locum" uncertain. Like Wilkinson, he rented rooms in London variously in Clifford's Inn and Dane's Court where he would be available at a moment's notice to accept any job that was going. The rooms were probably wretched enough, providing the barest refuge between engagements. Because his wife and children were unacceptable encumbrances to the practitioners who employed him, they lived on the south Kent coast, where Freeman visited them whenever he could find the opportunity. This entire period of Freeman's life is still obscure but some hints of the facts can be found in the present series. Did he, we wonder, go as far afield as the Wash a hundred miles north of London, as Wilkinson was glad to do?

The bitterness of these years never forsook Freeman as several passages in the early Thorndyke novels reveal. But in Pitcairn's hands – for it was he who fashioned all the Ashdown stories in accordance with the themes provided by his partner – the bitterness has evaporated and been replaced by a sense of adventure and excitement. It was "J J" who also provided the strong cycling motif in the stories; in this first great era of the British two-wheeler it was he who took to the small saddle, while Freeman preferred "Shanks' pony."

The stories, though slight, are pleasantly varied. Usually a patient, but in two cases the practitioner himself, is the centre of the mystery. Except in the first story, set on Freeman's home turf at Hampstead, the background is the English countryside at the turn of the century. As we observe our hero pedalling vigorously mile upon mile, day in and day out, to visit his far-flung patients, we are reminded once again that the lives, health and well-being of the rural population seventy years ago, especially in districts blessed by the services of a devoted and intelligent physician, were certainly no less secure than those of the sick and aging who nowadays may often lie untended within a stone's throw of computerized palaces of advanced medical technology.

Norman Donaldson
October 1975

*For further details of the two authors and their relationship, see my *In Search of Dr Thorndyke* (Bowling Green University Popular Press, Bowling Green, Ohio, 1971) and introductory material in Clifford Ashdown's *The Further Adventures of Romney Pringle* and *The Queen's Treasure*, both published by Oswald Train.

# The Adventure at Heath Crest

"I'm sure my husband would prefer you not to cycle much, Dr Wilkinson. It's quite true you are in the country as soon as you get over the Heath, and out there, of course, it doesn't matter so much; but the Hampstead patients are all carriage people, and I know they wouldn't like their doctor to call on a bicycle."

"Oh, I quite understand the point, Mrs Walland," I replied. "I only mentioned it with the idea of getting a little exercise when I went out to Finchley, and so on."

"I am confident my husband's interests will be safe in your hands," said the lady majestically. "With a high-class practice like this one cannot be too circumspect; there is so much jealousy among the successful practitioners."

Dr Walland was attending the International Medical Congress at Vienna. He had not impressed me as being an ardent scientist, but then, as everybody knows, these gatherings are only a species of superior picnics, and Vienna, too, is the gayest capital in the world.

Poor man! A very short stay in the house enlightened me as to his motives. Mrs Walland early remarked that it was only her dread of the Channel, and her fear of what might befall the household in her absence, that had prevented her accompanying her husband; and after but a very few hours of her society I felt sure that the Congress had commended itself to Walland by the distance it put between them. But the solid fee I was earning by the charge of an equally solid practice was some compensation for all I had to suffer in Mrs Walland's society.

1

I may remark that I had had a not unsuccessful career at the hospital. As soon as I was qualified I had filled the usual staff appointments of house-surgeon and house-physician, which, at a hospital like Bart's, it is no small honour to have held. But when my two years of work were finished, I found that my troubles were only beginning. There were no more scholarships open to me, even if I could have afforded the time to work up for them; my mother's income was sufficient for herself alone, and I steadily set my face against her repeated offer to realise a small portion of her small capital for me to buy a practice with.

As to this, there is no more speculative investment than the purchase of a practice. I should never have felt comfortable had any portion of my mother's income depended upon my success or failure, especially as I had had so little experience of private practice – little more, indeed, than was derived from sitting in the consulting room of my old friend, Nosbury, on an occasional evening when he went courting, and either repeating his prescriptions, or staving off those patients who consented to see me with a "placebo" calculated to last them until the day after tomorrow. So, in default of anything more permanent, I determined to go in for what are called *locums* for the time being.

It must have been about the third day after I took up the work that I was sent for to "Heath Crest." I remember the morning well. I had gone after breakfast to a patient of the poorer class out at Hendon, which was about the periphery of Walland's district, and enjoyed a glorious free-wheel first down the Bishop's Avenue and then, after a short pull up the North Road, down again by way of Finchley, and passing the house on my way over the Heath I felt a longing to examine it from the inside.

It was not for any great beauty it possessed, for of architectural grace it had little, standing four square behind its railing-spears as baldly as a block of unpolished granite. But I was taken by the prim old garden stretching for quite a considerable way beside the road, with a cedar showing above the wall, and especially by just a glimpse of the delicately fluted columns and double fan-light of the doorway in the Adam style.

Mrs Walland was out when the message came, or doubtless I should have had a minute history of Mr Fahbwerker, his business, his income and his wife – especially his wife. But, as it happened, this was spared me, and when I tapped the brass knocker at Heath Crest I knew nothing of the patient I was about to see.

The house was luxuriously, even magnificently, furnished. My steps fell noiselessly on the ankle-deep rugs as I crossed the hall and was shown into a room on the ground floor, where a lady with fluffy yellow hair awaited me. She appeared nervous and agitated as she explained she was Mrs Fahbwerker, that she had sent for me on account of her husband, and would I sit down while she told me something about him? She related how he was a financier, had been much troubled over affairs on the Gold Coast where he had large business interests, had lately become sleepless and subject to fainting attacks. Dr Walland had said he might die in one of them. Did I think that excessive worry would be likely to cause them? etc., etc. She seemed, indeed, to carry a perfect diary of her husband's symptoms in her head, so much so that when I expressed a wish to see the patient for myself she continued her history all the way upstairs, and even into the sick-room.

Mr Fahbwerker was certainly very ill, and when I came to examine him I could make allowances for even a greater degree of excitement than his wife displayed. Cold and almost pulseless, his every movement seemed feeble. Although he was quite conscious, his voice was no more than a hoarse whisper; but, strange to say, I could find not the slightest reason for this alarming state of things, which appeared to be due to heart-failure pure and simple. In any case, his condition was most critical, and I lost no time in giving him a hypodermic injection of ether and prescribing some hot strong coffee. He was so far gone that he took a considerable time to rally. I even thought at one time of applying electricity to the heart, and it was quite an hour before I felt justified in leaving him.

When I got back Mrs Walland had kept luncheon waiting. She was most curious as to what had detained me, and appeared quite nettled at my reticence. Although she returned again and again to the subject I managed to stave off her inquisitiveness, and at length, finding me inexorable, she ceased to catechise me. I have always made it a point (in common with any other man worthy of professional confidence) to refuse to discuss the affairs of patients with those outside their immediate circle. From her behaviour on this occasion, I feared that Mrs Walland was accustomed to find her husband more pliable.

In the course of the afternoon I took the opportunity of being close by to look in again at Heath Crest. I found the patient fairly comfortable. Although he had been taking a prescription I ordered in the morning, Mrs Fahbwerker told me that he had had another, although a slighter, attack not long before.

I must confess that he puzzled me very much. As to the reality of his peril when I first saw him there could be no question; but now that he had mended he presented not the slightest sign of disease. Similar attacks are not unknown to arise from acute dyspepsia, but scarcely to such a dangerous extent as this. Besides, I could find nothing of the sort about him. For the rest he was a fine, well-built man, of the florid German type, in the prime of life. I could really advise little more than to continue the treatment and to keep plenty of stimulants at hand.

On my way downstairs I could not resist stopping to admire the magnificent view from the windows. On the one side was the Heath, with its glorious avenue of chestnuts merging in the woods, which stretched unbroken across the Weald to Harrow; on the other, its huge basin rimmed by the heights of Surrey, spread London, with St Paul's and Westminster showing like islands above the grey perpetual haze. I turned to congratulate Mrs Fahbwerker, perhaps injudiciously, on so priceless an outlook; but she did not seem to notice my remark, asking me the senseless question which stirs in me fresh resentment every time I hear it:

"Is there any danger, doctor?"

I took refuge in the historical reply of the physician – a mythical one, for aught I know, but it always satisfies:

"Illness is always dangerous."

I was in the thick of seeing patients that evening when there came an urgent message to visit Mr Fahbwerker, and then, right on the heels of it, a second one to say that he was dead! I had not time to reflect upon it at the moment, but about an hour afterwards Mrs Fahbwerker came herself; she said she had called for the death certificate. She did not seem very greatly distressed, and it occurred to me that perhaps the event so long threatened when it did come at last had been rather a relief in view of the perpetual alarm in which she must have been living of late. As I was momentarily expecting a distinguished literary man who was coming by appointment to be examined for life insurance, it was a relief to find her in so slightly sentimental a mood.

While I dashed off the certificate she told me all about the fatal attack, of its sudden onset, and of its fatal ending before any remedies could take effect. As I have said, I was desperately busy; and as the literary man arrived, for a wonder, punctually to his time, I was very glad to see the back of Mrs Fahbwerker.

I made a strange discovery when the insurer succeeded the widow. I do not mean to imply that there was anything very remarkable in a literary man insuring his life, but I discovered that Walland did a very fair amount of insurance work. When I picked up the book in which he laboriously noted the results of his examinations, it opened at a page on which the name Fahbwerker was prominent. Running through the entry I found it to be the patient who had just died. Walland had passed him as a first-class life, the value of the insurance being five thousand pounds, and, most significant fact of all, the date of the examination was a bare six weeks ago!

I hope the literary man was not unfavourably impressed with the manner in which I examined him, but as I gave him a clean bill of health he had little cause to complain. The fact is, I was so astounded with what I had just read concerning Fahbwerker that I could think of little else; and when at the close of the evening's work I learned that

Mrs Walland had gone out to a concert, I felt inexpressibly thankful at the opportunity to think over my discovery in quiet.

That a man who only six weeks ago was in the best of health should suddenly and without cause develop an acute form of heart disease which proved rapidly fatal, was certainly remarkable. I was still worrying over the mystery, when there came an urgent call elsewhere. As I cycled past Heath Crest and glanced up at the windows, with never a glimmer of light in any of them, I regretted the lateness of the hour which alone prevented me from calling on Mrs Fahbwerker so that I might clear up some of the doubts which troubled me.

My visit was to a poor creature in the last stage of phthisis. When I got to the house I found there had been profuse haemorrhage from the lungs, and was annoyed to find that in the luxury of attending to Fahbwerker that morning the very drug which I now wanted to use must have dropped from my pocket hypodermic case. At least the tiny bottle was missing, and as the patient was practically bleeding to death, I ran on to Walland's chemist, who was fortunately close at hand.

"I hear that Mr Fahbwerker died tonight," observed the chemist.

I had replenished my case, and was about to hurry back, when the remark, made with all the urbanity of the man's calling, arrested me; for, in spite of my present errand, the dead man was still uppermost in my thoughts.

"Yes, it was rather sudden," I admitted.

"I can't say I am altogether surprised," observed the chemist.

"Why? He always had very good health," said I, ingenuously.

"Yes; but look at the way he was always drugging himself."

"Drugging himself?"

"Yes. Why, there was hardly a day that Mrs Fahbwerker wasn't in here for something or other for him."

"Indeed? What sort of drugs?"

"Oh, antipyrin principally."

"Did she say what she wanted it for?"

"She was always talking about the dreadful headaches her husband used to have, and I was always warning her against antipyrin."

As I listened, I was conscious of a species of vertigo, so impetuous was the rush of ideas; but, recovering myself, I bade the chemist a hasty "good night," and ran back to the patient.

All the way along, the rays of every street-lamp seemed to form the word "antipyrin." When I bared the patient's arm the blue veins traced it on the skin; when I looked away the lines of the hideous wall-paper grouped to spell it there also; and later on, when I had climbed wearily to bed, I still saw it through my closed eyelids.

Yes, it was all plain enough now that it had been too late to save him. Fahbwerker must have been killed by an overdose of antipyrin – perhaps the most fatally depressing drug known to medicine. The symptoms were conclusive, and I marvelled how so simple a case could have puzzled me so much.

After a night during which I hardly slept an hour altogether, I rose early, intending to call on Mrs Fahbwerker and explain her criminal folly in assisting her husband in his lavish phyicking. I also wanted to get the death certificate from her before she had registered it, since it was clear there would have to be an inquest. One thing after another conspired to delay me, and it had gone noon before I reached Heath Crest. The place looked very sombre with its drawn blinds, and the servant spoke in the hushed voice peculiar to a household which death has visited.

She was doubtful whether Mrs Fahbwerker would see me; her mistress was at home to no one, but she would see if the prohibition extended to me. In a few minutes she returned and showed me to a room, where, indeed, I could hear the voice of Mrs Fahbwerker as she greeted me, although her figure was a mere suggestion in the gloom of the drawn blinds.

"I am sorry to intrude upon you at such a time, Mrs Fahbwerker," said I, "but I am afraid I shall have to withdraw the death certificate I gave you last night."

"I don't quite understand you, doctor," came the voice from the other side of the room, with just a little tremor in the tones.

"I have been thinking the matter over, and the certificate no longer expresses my conscientious opinion as to the cause of Mr Fahbwerker's death."

There was no answer, but I caught the sound of her rapid breathing.

"I was very puzzled all along by your husband's illness," I continued, "and if I had been less busy when you called last night, or if I had had longer to think over it, I should have declined to give you a certificate."

Still no answer but Mrs Fahbwerker's dress rustled greatly, as if she experienced some emotion.

"To speak plainly," I went on after another pause, "I am satisfied that Mr Fahbwerker's death was not due to natural causes. What I should like to know now is this – was he in the habit of taking drugs?"

"Never!" The retort was sharp and vicious as the crack of a rifle.

"You never knew him to take medicine without advice?"

"Never!"

"Antipyrin, for instance?"

"Certainly not! Why are you asking all these questions?"

"Because I found no sign of disease about Mr Fahbwerker. He ought not to have died, and I can only account for it by his misuse of some drug such as antipyrin."

"He never took it – I am sure of it!"

"You have taken it yourself, perhaps?"

"No – that is, I have occasionally – a long time ago."

"It is very strange," I remarked with meaning.

"It *is* strange, doctor. Why didn't you tell me all this before? You have deceived me!"

"I have done nothing of the sort, Mrs Fahbwerker."

"Yes; you certified the death was due to heart-failure."

"I have altered my opinion, and I have come to tell you that I withdraw the certificate."

"Why?"

"Because there must be an inquest."

I could hear the swish of her dress as she suddenly rose; she was evidently very agitated.

I had no wish to have a scene with her, so I determined to close the interview.

"Can I see the body?" I asked. It occurred to me that it would be as well to do so before I laid the facts before the coroner.

"No! It is impossible."

"Really, Mrs Fahbwerker, I must protest against this! No one can regret more than I do that there has been any unpleasantness, but I put it to you whether you are not acting very injudiciously in refusing to let me, as your husband's medical attendant, view the body – if only to certify the fact of death."

"The coffin is screwed down."

"The coffin!" I exclaimed.

"I wish the funeral to be as soon as possible."

I felt that Mrs Fahbwerker was too strong for me. Why this haste, I wondered. There was no reason for it on sanitary or any other grounds that I could imagine. I knew not what to think of it all. But one thing I saw clearly; although she had practically defied me, Mrs Fahbwerker could not stop my communicating with the coroner, and, determined to play my trump-card at once, I took a very frigid leave of her.

An idea occurred to me at the hall door, and I inquired the undertaker's address of the servant. It was only in the High Street, and I was lucky enough to find him in.

"I am Dr Wilkinson. I attended Mr Fahbwerker on behalf of Dr Walland," I explained.

The man bowed.

"You are hurrying on the funeral," I suggested.

"I understood the lady to say it was by the doctor's advice."

"Not mine!" I declared.

"Well, sir, we only had the order last night, but we delivered the coffin this morning – we're used to emergencies."

"And you screwed the body down at once."

"Oh, no, sir!"

"Mrs Fahbwerker said the coffin was screwed down, and that was the reason I couldn't see the body."

"Some mistake," said the undertaker incredulously.

"She certain said so to me only a few minutes ago."

"Well, all I can say, sir, is that they must have done it themselves! I know nothing about it. Why, you know, sir, it's never done till the very last."

"When is the funeral to be, then?"

"I wrote by Mrs Fahbwerker's orders to the Necropolis at once, but I don't expect an answer before tomorrow at the soonest."

"Necropolis! Is the funeral to be there, then?"

"The lady said it was her husband's wish, and the doctor advised haste."

I suppressed an exclamation.

"It was you who gave the certificate, wasn't it, sir?"

"Oh, yes, I gave the certificate," and as I left the shop I inwardly exclaimed, "and bitterly do I regret it!"

I wanted to be alone, and the society of Mrs Walland being unfavourable to reflection, I made a detour in the opposite direction, and striding across the Heath, sat for a little time in the Vale of Health to think seriously over the situation.

Here was the procuring of quantities of a dangerous drug, its employment with fatal result, then hurried funeral preparations, a refusal to allow any examination of the body, and lastly the hurried interment – of course, to effectually destroy all evidence of foul play. Even the sordid motive was not lacking in the insurance which poor Fahbwerker had just effected on his life.

As the full horror of the crime burst upon me I set off homeward at a run. I felt I could not rest until I had set an inquiry going.

Suddenly I recalled Mrs Fahbwerker's statement that Walland had predicted the fatal termination. Could I have judged her too hastily?

I hurried to the consulting room the moment I got in, and hunted through the case-book; there was not a word of Fahbwerker since the entry concerning the life insurance. I turned up the daybook and then the visiting list, with equal unsuccess. Could Walland – methodical and careful as I knew him to be – have omitted all reference to such a matter? Incredible! Then this, too, could only be one more in the long string of falsehoods uttered by Mrs Fahbwerker, whom I now regarded as a callous assassin.

I was too much worried and upset to have any appetite for lunch, so, leaving an apology to Mrs Walland with the servant, I started for the coroner's office. I calculated to reach there about three, and in order to lose no time, I took some paper with me, and busied myself while in the train by writing a full and complete statement with the aid of my fountain pen.

As I feared, both the coroner and his deputy were engaged at inquests, but I left my statement with an official who promised to bring it to the coroner's notice as soon as possible, and to let me know the result by evening.

It was a great relief when I had got this disagreeable business over, and satisfied that I had now put a substantial spoke in Mrs Fahbwerker's wheel, I spent a busy afternoon in picking up the loose threads of the day's work which she and her affairs had somewhat disorganised.

As was only natural, the coroner quite took my view of the case, and in the course of the evening I was waited on by one of his officers with a summons to the inquest he would hold the day after next, and an authority for me to make a post-mortem examination. The officer told me he was on his way to serve a similar summons on Mrs Fahbwerker, with an order to deliver up the body for removal to the mortuary forthwith. I knew I had a very busy day before me, so I took the opportunity of sending word by the officer that I would hold the post-mortem the next morning at eight. I felt that I had now done all that was possible to assist the ends of justice, and seized an early opportunity of going to bed after a day that had certainly not been the least harrowing of my life.

I rose early, and, snatching a hasty breakfast, cycled down to the coroner's court. It was a little before eight when I arrived, but although the mortuary keeper had everything in readiness, there was no corpse. However, just as eight struck, it arrived in charge of the coroner's officer and the undertaker.

"Wouldn't Mrs Fahbwerker give up possession?" I asked him.

"Why, no, sir; she never gave herself the chance," said he, with a grin.

"What on earth do you mean?"

"Why, when I left you, sir, I went and served Mrs Fahbwerker with the notice, and said I should want to take charge of the body this morning. She gave me the address of the undertaker here, and I went and arranged with him. Well, it seems that I had hardly got out of the house before she took and packed up all her boxes, and sent out for a cab and drove away, and no one's set eyes on her since."

"Where did she go to?" I was profoundly interested in this new development, which simply confirmed my worst suspicions.

"The maids say she told the cabman to go to Hampstead Station, but that must have been a blind, for she couldn't take all her luggage by that line, and when they got there she must have told the cabman to drive somewhere else."

"What time was that?"

"About half-past ten, they said."

Scarcely time, I reflected, to get to the Continent; she would have to wait till this morning.

"And you found the body all right?" I asked.

For answer he slapped his hand on the coffin.

"Well, I suppose it will save a lot of scandal if she manages to get away," I observed. "After all, it's the affair of the police."

"Ha, sir! I tell you there's a lot more behind it," said the coroner's officer, mysteriously. "Strikes me it's going to be one of the rummiest affairs I've ever took a part in, and that's saying a good deal, I can tell you."

"How?" I thought he alluded to the murder, and was anxious to know how much had leaked out by this time.

"Well, sir, I can't help laughing, but it's just this way. As I was leaving the house after serving the notice I stopped to tell the servant we should be there about half-past seven, and I was just walking away when who should I see coming up the front path, as hard as he could pelt, but Sergeant Brown, from Scotland Yard, whom I knew from often seeing him at these affairs.

" 'Why, what do *you* want?' says I. 'This is none of your business yet awhile; we haven't had our say yet.'

" 'What do you mean?' says he. 'I've got a warrant to serve.'

" 'Warrant?' says I. 'Who for?'

" 'Mr Fahbwerker,' says he, mysterious like; 'and where's the joke?' For he saw I was laughing fit to split myself.

" 'You're a day too late,' says I.

" 'What's that?' says he, quite startled.

" 'Someone else has been arresting him before you,' I says jokingly.

" 'Nonsense,' he says, 'there's no other warrant out against him but the one I've got.'

" 'Oh, yes,' I says, 'there is.'

" 'What d'ye mean?' he says.

" 'A death warrant,' I says.

" 'Get out,' he says, 'you're joking.'

" 'Not a bit of it,' says I; 'if you don't believe me, just go and ask at the house.'

" 'You don't say so,' says he, struck all of a heap like. 'You're quite sure, are you,' he asks presently.

" 'All I know,' says I, 'is there's going to be an inquest, and I've just served them with the summons to attend, and the body's going to the mortuary tomorrow morning for the doctor to make a post-mortem examination.' "

I said nothing, but I suppose my astonishment must have been palpable, and the officer continued:

"I tell you, sir, it was just about the best thing could have happened to the poor fellow to die when he did, though I don't suppose he'd agree with me if he could speak."

"What did the detective do?" I asked presently.

"Oh, of course he didn't want to go into the house and make a fuss and upset everybody after what I told him, but he said he'd like to come down here and just inspect the body this morning, so as he could make an official report why the warrant wasn't executed. Ah! Here he is! Good morning, sergeant."

Time was getting on, so as soon as the detective had been admitted I told the undertaker to open the coffin and he set to work with his screwdriver. I noticed that although he used a brace and centre-bit apparatus, he seemed to have a good deal of trouble getting the screws out; Mrs Fahbwerker must have driven them in with the strength of desperation. She was certainly a clever and resourceful woman.

At length all the screws were extracted, and while the mortuary keeper pushed the lid aside, the undertaker plucked off the underlying sheet.

For a second or two we all gazed stupidly at one another, and then the detective went down on his hands and knees and rapidly strewed the floor with about a hundred-weight of coal and several large books, which were the only contents of the coffin!

It was the coroner's officer who first broke the silence. "Well," he chuckled, "this would have been a good funeral! Have you got your warrant, sergeant? You'll need a coal-van to take your prisoner in."

The laugh (half hysterical from myself) which we all found for the witticism was an unspeakable relief to my nerves, for so long at their highest tension.

"Yes, I've got it," replied the detective grimly, "and, what's more, I mean to execute it. But, between the lot of you, you've given him twelve hours start of me! Did you measure the body?" he asked of the undertaker.

"Only under the sheet," the latter admitted. "He seemed stiff enough then, but I wasn't in the room a couple of minutes."

"You never saw the body either, did you, doctor?"

"No," I replied. "Mrs Fahbwerker came and told me he was dead just when I was very busy and only too glad to get rid of her by giving her the certificate. When I wanted to see the body the next day, she told me the coffin was screwed down."

"A clever dodge, certainly, if it had come off," was Brown's comment.

"But where can he be?" I exclaimed.

"Waiting for his wife on the other side of the Channel, most likely. What's the time now? Eight-thirty. There's time yet! Good morning, gentlemen," and the door slammed on the detective.

The coroner's officer advised me to call and see the coroner "as soon as possible," but it was late in the afternoon before I was able to get to the office and make a rather shame-faced explanation. As I left a paper-boy outside was howling: "Mysterious affair at Hampstead!" and in some trepidation I bought an evening paper. I ran my eye down the pink column, but this was all I read:

## SENSATIONAL AFFAIR
## ARREST OF A DEAD MAN AT DOVER.

Our Dover correspondent wires that Mr Julius Fahbwerker, late of Old Broad Street, and well known in financial circles, was arrested this morning when about to go on board the Ostend boat. Mr Fahbwerker, who was accompanied by his wife, was taken into custody by the local police and detained until the arrival of Detective Sergeant Brown from London, who had the warrant for his arrest.

We understand that it was reported in the city yesterday that Mr Fahbwerker was dead, and inquiries at his residence, Heath Crest, Hampstead, confirmed the statement. Information which our representatives succeeded in obtaining on the spot puts a very sensational aspect on the affair. It appears that preparations were in active progress for a funeral when they were abruptly stopped by the order of the coroner, whose authority had been invoked by certain friends of the family, and arrangements were even made for a post-mortem examination, when it was found that no corpse was forthcoming. As the case is *sub judice* we refrain from any comment upon the extraordinary circumstances, which have naturally created the most profound sensation in the city.

Yes, as the detective had observed, it was certainly a clever dodge. Although I could not help seeing I had been made a fool of, yet it was undeniable that any medical man might have been deceived by such a carefully prepared train of symptoms.

Fahbwerker, when his arrest was impending, must have resolved to disappear, and doubtless experimented until he had found the utmost dose of antipyrin he thought he could take with safety. But he had nearly overdone it – a very little more and he would have killed himself in reality.

The Fahbwerkers had probably considered Walland's absence as their golden opportunity, and from my apparent inexperience were unprepared for my insistence on viewing the body, a course which they evidently knew I was under no legal obligation to take. After all, I should never have done this, and the bogus funeral might have been held, if it had not been for the accident which led me to the chemist's shop.

# How I Acted for an Invalid Doctor

"I think you'll like the berth at Crowham," said Adamson, the medical agent, as I stood in his office. "It's not a large fee, but Dr Ringmer says there's very little doing, and if it hadn't been for his club practice he wouldn't have taken the trouble to get a *locum* down at all as he hopes to be up and about again in a week."

It was a curious coincidence that although I had hardly heard of the place before, on my way to Waterloo the next day I caught sight of the name on the contents bill of a newspaper. From all accounts it was far too sleepy a little town to make any figure in the world, but at the station I got an evening paper, and there it was, sure enough.

It appeared there had lately been a series of burglaries in the neighbourhood, and some comment had been made on the fact that they had all taken place in the middle of the night, and not, as is usual in the case of attempts on country houses, during the dinner hour. The burglars were believed to be members of an expert gang, and so persistent and daring had they become that a regular panic seemed to have sprung up round about the place. After all, the news did not interest me much; I had no valuables to lose. But as the train was slow, even for a southern railway, I had plenty of time to learn all that was said on the subject before I arrived at Crowham.

As there was no one to meet me at the station I left my bag in the cloak-room, and cycled up through the town. Dr Ringmer had said, according to Adamson, that he did much of his work on a cycle, and

17

the "CTC" road-book spoke highly of the going thereabouts. The station-master had directed me to the house opposite the fire-station.

"You can't miss it; it's a straight road," said he. So it was, but he forgot to add that it was a sharp down-grade all the way. Although I jammed on the brake the machine nearly ran away with me, and I had shot by the fire-station before I noticed it. Something was wrong with the brake; damaged in the train, I concluded.

I dismounted at the foot of the hill and had a weary push up again. The doctor's house contrasted with its neighbours, which were nearly all roughcast and timbered, being of a neat red brick with a three-windowed front, the central opening on each floor a blank, reminiscent of the days of Mr Pitt's window-tax. There was a coach house at the side, and as I drew up a man came out and touched his forelock.

"Are you Dr Wilkinson, sir?" as he took the machine from me. "I'd have met you at the station, but the doctor didn't know what train you were coming by."

When I got inside I was quite charmed with the house. It was such a queer old rambling place, full of long, crooked passages, with every now and then a step just when you least expected it. There could be no doubt as to its age, for the doors and windows were so palpably out of plumb as to give one the impression of a rolling ship.

I found myself straddling for my sea legs as I stood in the middle of the consulting room. Although the floor fell uncannily it was firm as a rock, for a large safe occupied the whole of one recess by the chimney.

There were plenty of book-cases about too, and while waiting I amused myself by estimating Dr Ringmer's literary taste. It seemed to be a very light one: of medical books there were next to none, but I found any number of the latest works on general science, and an enormous quantity of fiction. In fact, novels were everywhere, and the works of Gaboriau and Boisgobey, authors whose acquaintance I had yet to make, were specially prominent.

"The doctor is sorry to have to ask you to step up to his room, but he is still rather poorly," said the housekeeper presently.

As I followed the woman upstairs I was struck with the solidity of the woodwork, but the stairs themselves were so warped, and continued to creak so long after they were trodden upon, that I twice looked back to see if someone were not following. If the house was not haunted it certainly ought to have been.

I found Dr Ringmer in bed in a back room on the first floor. As the light from the declining sun struck in upon him I had a full view of a handsome, clean-shaven face, reminding me of a bust of one of the Roman emperors, and lying there with the neck of his sleeping-suit carelessly open, I could see that he had the torso of a Hercules.

"Sorry to make you come up," he remarked pleasantly; "but I suppose you are used to mounting stairs." He gave me a large, well-shaped hand, which gripped mine firmly.

"You'll find this more like hospital work than anything else," he continued. "I've got a very small list at present, and most of those can wait till I am better. You'll principally have to see the clubbers – I hope you don't feel a draught, by the way; I always keep the windows open."

The abrupt remark made me turn to the windows, when, for the first time, I noticed a curious thing. Each was a light of twelve little old-fashioned panes, and they were flung open as far as they would go. An absolute forest of Virginia creeper and wild-rose festooned across them, and sturdy ropes had insinuated themselves between, throwing out trailers into the bed-room, while one of quite respectable size was actually extending itself along the floor. The windows must have remained open night and day for months past!

"Quite tropical, isn't it?" said Ringmer, without waiting for me to reply. "You'll find the garden pleasant to sit in, with plenty of fruit if you care for that sort of thing. Just take a look at it."

I got up and walked to the window. What a garden! There seemed no end to it. First there was a long stretch of lawn with a hot-house on one side, and grapes clustering thickly inside, and further on a mossy walk between a perfect forest of old-fashioned flowers, hollyhocks, and sunflowers and honeysuckle to any amount, and beyond them again fruit trees.

Such trees! Apple trees, pear trees, plum trees, mulberry trees, with figs, currants, and raspberry bushes between. The whole was bounded, as to the side at least, for I was quite unable to see to the end, with a good honest old red-brick wall, thick and buttressed and lichenous. It did my heart good to see how warmly it glowed in the sun. I don't know how long I remained looking in delight; I forgot that I was not alone until I heard Ringmer's voice.

"Yes, it's a glorious garden." I started, for I had said nothing, although he read my thoughts. "Yes, as you say, it's glorious," he repeated; "although you'd get very sick of it if you had to live here always."

"Never!" I exclaimed emphatically.

He smiled.

"Do you cycle?" he asked presently.

I told him how I had brought the machine down with me.

"That's right," he said. "You'll find the roads first-rate; you'd almost think they had been sandpapered; and dry as a bone too. You see, the soil is sandy, and the rain soaks in at once. By the by, you must be careful if you ride out after dark; the police are beastly keen about lamps being lit up, I can tell you. Cave – my man, you know – mostly rides my machine; I haven't been on it for a long time now."

"Have you been ill long?" I ventured to ask. The fact was I was getting desperately curious as to the nature of his complaint, and seized on the opening he gave me to ask him. Ever since I came into the room I had been watching him narrowly; but for the life of me I was unable to see the least sign of anything amiss with him.

"Oh, this cursed malaria – West Africa, you know." He pointed to the table by the bed-side, on which a large bottle of quinine tabloids was standing. "I'm better just now." Which was certainly true, for his skin was quite cool and moist when I shook hands with him.

"It's an obstinate complaint, certainly," I remarked. "You never know when the germs are going to wake up again."

"Yes, indeed it is! I took a ship out to Accra seven or eight years ago, and then was fool enough to go up country a bit. I thought I was tolerably proof, but I caught a dose of 'black water,' and very nearly joined the majority. However, I pulled through, thanks to what is known as a sound constitution." He thrust a muscular arm into the air and surveyed it absently, running a caressing finger over the cord-like muscles.

I was pondering what to say next when, "Just ring the bell, will you?" he said, adding when the housekeeper appeared, "Show Dr Wilkinson his room, and send Cave down to the station to fetch the doctor's bag. Seven o'clock will suit you for dinner, I suppose? I'll try and have a nap now, if you'll excuse me."

My room, I found, was immediately above Ringmer's, with the same kind of creeper growing outside, but although running higher than the windows it did not obstruct them. Looking out I was able to see to the end of the garden, which was quite as wild as the part nearer to the house.

Ringmer, I discovered, was a bit of a mechanic. After dining in solitary state (a meal admirably cooked, by the way; he possessed a genius in Mrs Carpenter!), I went to have a look at my cycle. I felt uneasy about it; to ride with a brake in that condition was to court disaster.

Cave had put the machine in an outhouse where Ringmer kept his own cycle, and, better still, his lathe. I soon found the reason of the brake's failure. As I expected, the damage had been done in the railway van, the lever being bent so as to lose half its power. I have always prided myself on being a practical cyclist, so it was not long before I had the whole affair off, and a very little gentle persuasion from Ringmer's vice soon put it right again. Mrs Carpenter saw fit to assist at the operation. I did not object, partly because I was unaware of her exact status in the establishment, partly because I was nervous of using another man's tools, and she was witness that I did them no damage.

No patients arriving, I seized the opportunity to do one or two small jobs about the machine, straightening a bent spoke, fitting a new washer to a valve, and finally oiled the bearings.

All the time Mrs Carpenter talked. I honestly think she was about the greatest talker I have ever met. She had been told it was a very fine lathe; the ironmonger said it had cost a lot of money. My cycle must have cost a lot too. She had heard they sold for as much as five pounds in the town. The doctor used to ride a lot on his machine; he always took it at nights, and never called up the groom. There had been a lot of night-work lately, no wonder he was laid up. He was a real clever man, and very handy with tools; many was the hour he used to spend in his workshop; and when the talk of these burglaries first came about he took and altered the locks on the consulting-room door and had a safe in, and fitted it into the wall himself, to keep his money and valuables in. Ah, he was a clever man! And then *da capo* with variations.

About half-way through with my work I happened to drop a nut, and, of course, it must needs conceal itself in the accumulation of dust and turnings under the lathe, so that I was nearly ten minutes hunting for it Ringmer was certainly very careless with his tools, for I raked out a new file and a perfectly good chuck from the heap.

Just before I found the nut, I turned up a twisted thing formed out of a single piece of very stout wire. I had never seen anything like it before, and it was so odd-looking that I was about to ask Mrs Carpenter if she knew what it was used for, when it occurred to me that it was just the thing I wanted for a tyre-lever. So, telling myself that it was of no value, I put it in my tool-bag incontinently.

It was getting dusk when I finished, so, Mrs Carpenter having disappeared and patients still declining to arrive, I had a look about the business part of the premises. The consulting-room I had already seen, and wondered at; but the surgery was an even greater surprise. At this distance of time I may be mistaken, but I think I was unable to count more than a dozen bottles of drugs in the place.

I peeped into a cupboard, thinking that Ringmer might be morbidly sensitive on the score of poisons, but it only sheltered a few empties. On the shelf just above the desk were some four or five "stock" mixtures, and scattered about here and there in any old corner were a few of the commoner drugs in daily use, a mere handful, making up the bare dozen I remember.

The day-book, too, was a most eccentric compilation. So far as I could understand Ringmer's hieroglyphics, there was no record of a single prescription. Indeed, it was impossible to see what work was actually done, as there was nothing recorded against the days, let alone the laborious nights of which Mrs Carpenter had spoken.

But if I marvelled at the drugs, I was simply astonished at the collection of instruments! I had opened several drawers without discovering more than willow chip-boxes, corks, and the odds and ends one expects to find; and there only remained to explore a mahogany nest of drawers, much neater and cleaner than anything else in the place, which stood in a dark corner.

At first I thought it locked, but when I gently touched the hinged flap which secured the whole nest I found it was open. The upper and narrower drawers were filled with papers, which I was careful not to disturb; and it was not until half-way down that I came on what I was seeking.

As I expected, the instruments were not in very good order. Indeed, they had been grossly neglected and I had made a resolution that if the work continued as slack as it promised to be, I would put in a little time at polishing them up and generally making them more worthy of their office. And here a most puzzling thing happened.

As I have said, it was only about half-way down the drawers that the instruments began — the usual assortment of knives and general tools for minor surgical work, all in very bad condition. But when I went lower I came upon the queerest looking set of things imaginable, the like of which I had never seen outside a museum of surgical instruments, and not even there! For if they were indeed surgical they must have belonged to some dead and gone era — the Saxon Heptarchy perhaps. None but a barbarian would nowadays use such things upon a human being.

They reminded me of veterinary instruments more than anything else. But those I knew they were not. I happen to know something about veterinary practice, as a fellow-student took it into his head there was more money to be made out of horses than men. Before he qualified as a "vet," I spent some very interesting mornings with him in Great College Street, Camden Town.

Quite characteristically, Ringmer seemed to keep his carpentering tools mixed up with the antiquities, and I noticed some drills, and even a collar from a lathe, jumbled together with them. The oddest thing of all with such a careless man was that the queer tools had not the slightest appearance of age, but were polished spick and span and without a particle of rust. Indeed, Ringmer seemed to think more of them than of his legitimate implements.

I was still puzzling over this extraordinary collection when I felt myself pushed roughly aside, and turning, saw Ringmer. He had come softly downstairs in his slippers and was now slapping in the drawers one after the other. I noticed particularly that, whether from agitation or fever, he was shaking all over.

"I shall be much obliged," he said, speaking in a high, sharp voice quite unlike his previous manner, "I shall be much obliged if, while you're down here, you won't go prying about."

I thought this a most ungentlemanly thing to say, and I took care to let him see I was offended.

"I am not in the habit of prying about, Dr Ringmer, and I have never been accused of such a thing before in my life! I was simply taking a look about the surgery, and found the instrument drawers unlocked."

"Well, I ask your pardon for what I said, but I keep some most important documents in those drawers, and I was upset at finding them open. I am feeling queer, and I really came down for the 'nepenthe.'" He carefully locked the flap-shutter, and then, taking the bottle from the shelf, poured a dose into a glass measure. "I hope you will make allowances for my miserable condition!" he said, and then disappeared silently with the draught.

Perhaps I am unduly sensitive, but, in spite of his apology, I still felt annoyed. As there was nothing doing, I went and sat in the basket-chair in the garden to cool down a bit. I lighted a pipe and watched the stars come out, but could not get over it. No doubt Ringmer felt seedy, but such a speech was quite uncalled for and I was still thinking of it when ten o'clock struck, and I came in and went to bed.

As a rule, I sleep soundly and dream seldom. But I suppose I was worried by the disagreeable events of the evening, for I continued to have queer dreams: as that Ringmer was seizing me in his muscular arms. Now I thought that he was throttling me, and another time that he was boring into me with one of those strange tools of his, and again that I was bound to his lathe and was being whirled round and round upon it. At last I began to dream that Ringmer was creeping in at the window with a tool in his hand to brain me as I slept, and that time I woke. As I sat up with the idea vividly in my recollection I distinctly heard the creeper rustling, as if someone were climbing up it.

I sprang out of bed and peered over the sill, for I had followed Ringmer's example and had opened both windows as wide as they would go. There was a faint light in the east, and I was able to see things fairly. Not a sound could I hear, but I was positive that the lower branches of the creeper were quivering, and a trailer or two on Ringmer's level were swinging, although there was no sign of a wind. Cats, I told myself; their flirtations had been going on all around me the whole time I sat in the garden.

I was roused again by a steam-saw getting to work in a timber yard. It was a glorious morning, and the sun was pouring into the room. I got up and dressed and went down through the still sleeping house into the garden.

At a nearer view it was not quite so attractive. The grass was long and in seed; the paths, too, sadly required weeding, and a number of sturdy wild flowers had sown themselves and were spreading in all directions. All the same, it was a very fine garden, and I calculated there must have been the best part of an acre within the walls. At the far end I discovered a door. The wood was very rotten and shaky, and at first I hesitated to draw the bolt, so rusty and stiff did it look. But it shot back easily, and I found myself standing in a narrow way which curved round to join the high road lower down.

As I closed the door again I noticed the tracks of a cycle leading into the garden. They were quite fresh on the damp ground, and I recognised the pattern of Ringmer's tyres. Strolling back, I looked in at the outhouse and there were the two cycles just as I had left them last evening. But, on glancing at Ringmer's tyres I saw patches of quite fresh mud upon them – indeed, in places it was still wet. Over in the stable Cave was whistling softly as he groomed his horse.

"Did it rain in the night?" I asked, leaning over the half-door.

"There was a bit of a sprinkle, I think, sir."

"Weren't you out in it, then?"

"Me, sir? Not I, thank goodness!"

"But didn't you take the cycle out?"

"Cycle out?" he repeated, eyeing me sharply. "I took no cycle out." I thought it best to change the subject.

"Roads are very good about here, aren't they?" I suggested.

"Very good indeed, sir."

As I went in to breakfast I wondered at the man's denial. The cycle had certainly been used, and no one but he could have ridden it. Why, then, did he lie about such a trifle?

"How is the doctor this morning?" I inquired as Mrs Carpenter brought in the breakfast.

"He's doing nicely, thank you, sir, and will be glad to see you when you're done."

I found Ringmer as genial as ever, and he made no allusion to the affair of the instrument cabinet. He had had a splendid night after the "nepenthe," he said, and thought if the work continued slack he would run down to Brighton for a week. There would only be one patient for me to visit, so far as he knew – the wife of the sergeant in charge of the police station. He had not seen her for a couple of days and she was doing so well that I should probably be able to strike her off the list altogether. I could cycle there, as it was only just at the other end of the town.

It occurred to me then to mention the cycle track I had seen at the gate. I felt that I ought to let him know, for if he went off as he proposed I should be in a way responsible for the household. I was very sorry I did so, however, for I had hardly spoken when he raised his fist, clenched tightly, and seemed about to flare out with something. But the mood passed, and he treated the matter lightly.

"Oh, it's that fellow Cave again," he laughed. "The fact is, he's after a girl at one of the houses in the neighbourhood, and since I gave him permission to use the cycle I suppose he finds it handy for a little early spooning. He's a good servant, and as good a fellow as ever stepped."

Although no one could have been more civil, it struck me that his manner was rather constrained after this. It might simply have been a reflection of his annoyance with Cave, although I thought he resented my interference. Anyhow, it was no further concern of mine.

One or two "clubbers" arrived after breakfast, whom I religiously dosed from the stock mixtures. Poor creatures, their faith in drugs was greater than mine!

It was nearing eleven when I started out on my visit to the police station. Crowham, I found, was not quite so small as it appeared at first. The principal street had numerous side ones branching off it, and turning up one I stumbled on the quaintest old market square. Here there was a curious round structure with benches running all round it for the village gossips to foregather – the "cage," as I learnt, now obsolete.

Its successor was at the farther end of town, and when I got there I found that Ringmer's forecast was correct and that the patient would need little more attention.

I had stood my cycle in the front garden of the little red-brick building, almost too pretty for a police station, and when I came out I was disgusted to find that the back tyre was nearly flat, the valve washer I had put in overnight having failed me. The sergeant, a true cyclist, lent a ready hand and between us we soon had the machine upside down, when I found, in addition, a thorn sticking tightly in the rubber.

I was commencing to remove the tyre with my fingers when I suddenly remembered my new lever, and fished it out of the tool-bag. The weather was warm, so I was not long waiting for the patch to stick; but when I replaced the tyre I found the reason the sergeant had left me to do the latter part of the process unassisted was his curious interest in my lever, which he was still examining intently.

"This is a queer sort of a tool," he remarked at last.

"Yes," said I. "Did you ever see one like it before?"

"Where did you come across it?" he asked, ignoring my question.

"In Crowham." I began to be impatient, and the sergeant's manner was just a trifle inquisitorial.

"Look here, sir," he continued apologetically; "I don't want to say anything to offend you, but do you mind telling me where you got it? It's not from curiosity I ask."

"In Dr Ringmer's workshop, if you must know."

He handed me back the lever without another word. But my own curiosity was raised, and I began to ask questions in my turn.

"Do you mind telling me what there is about it that interests you so much?"

He stepped back, and shut the door of the police station before he answered, in a low voice:

"If you'd found it anywhere else than where you did, sir, I should have said it was a picklock."

I suppose I must have looked my amazement, for he added emphatically: "I should, sir!"

Our conversation was cut short by the arrival of a constable with a sheaf of papers, and as I rode off I smiled to think what a mountain the man's professional instinct had raised from such a molehill. No doubt it was a picklock, since he said so; but what then? Ringmer was a mechanic, as I knew. And had not Mrs Carpenter spoken of his skill as a locksmith?

When I got back I found a far more important matter to think about. An urgent call had come from Paddenswick Castle. Ringmer seemed very excited over it, and, I learnt, had asked for me a dozen times.

"Look here!" he commenced, the moment I entered the room. "The Duke of Hammersmith is my best patient. It's just my luck to be laid up when I'm wanted – most likely he's got DT. There's a strain of hereditary alcoholism in the family, and he was drinking like a fish last week. You know, by the by, that there's no such thing in private practice, don't you?"

"Brain fever, you mean," I answered promptly.

"That's it. Well, you'll have to be as tactful as you can with the Duchess, who'll probably have hysteria if she finds the Duke has got 'em again. You know what hysteria is, too, I suppose?"

"Influenza!"

"Good. You know more about private practice than I gave you credit for. Well, hurry up, for goodness sake."

On the way out Cave dilated on the magnificence of Paddenswick. How the Duke had nearly drunk himself to death until he married Miss Hepzibah Mudross, daughter of the millionaire ironmaster of Pittsburgh, USA, and reformed. How the Duchess' diamonds were the talk of the country, and how she had so many that she even wore them to bed. And how a rumour had filtered through the police station that the house had been attempted by the burglars only last night. I asked him at length how he came to know so much about the family, and he answered – rather sheepishly, as I thought – that he knew one of the servants, at which I smiled.

When we arrived at the Castle I was hurried across a vast mausoleum of a hall and up a staircase, lined with portraits of dead and gone Hammersmiths, into a boudoir, where I found an agitated lady who nasally demanded the reason of Dr Ringmer's absence. It was a hard task to explain matters, and a little harder still to retain my footing. Indeed, just how I did it I cannot explain now, but whether through impudence or diplomacy I gradually led her on to a relation of the patient's symptoms, and was standing by his bedside within a quarter of an hour of my arrival.

There was no doubt about the "brain fever;" it was as bad a case as could well be. His Grace was struggling with four men-servants, who had all their work cut out to keep him on the bed; while as to his language, it was enough to make a pirate quail. There was only one thing to be done, so I waited till he had quieted down a bit, and then gave him a hypodermic injection of morphia. When I got away after a stay of over three hours he was enjoying the first sleep he had had for nearly a week.

After dinner, while I was smoking in the garden, Ringmer sent down for some "nepenthe," and when I took it up I told him all about the morning's adventures. He smacked his lips as much over the big fee he expected to get, perhaps, as over the "nepenthe," and leaving him a dose for the night, I turned in myself, horribly tired.

It seemed as if I had only just closed my eyes when the night-bell went off with the dismal cracked note of all its tribe – well do I know the sound! The speaking-tube was in Ringmer's room, so I had to go downstairs to the door. It was the Duke again. I could have sworn it.

As I passed Ringmer's door I listened for a second, and thought I detected a snore. I was glad he had not been roused, thanks to the "nepenthe." I had no wish to disturb Cave, so I took out the cycle, and lighting my lamp, got away through the garden-door without disturbing anybody.

I found the Duke very much awake. The "brain fever" had returned, so the Duchess informed me. Her confidence in me was obviously shaken, and I had to begin nearly all over again from the point I had started from in the morning. In the intervals of about an hour's catechism from the Duchess I had managed to get the Duke quieted down at last, and was congratulating myself on being able to make my escape. Suddenly a tremendous uproar arose on the discovery that the Duchess' apartments had been broken into. Most of the feminine portion of the household were in hysterics, but I was delighted to see that their mistress was too much concerned as to her jewellery to follow their example.

There was nothing more I could do, and as the Duchess in her excitement seemed not only to have forgotten her husband but myself as well, I seized the opportunity to retire quietly.

At the door I found my friend the police-sergeant, and stayed a moment to inquire as to the truth of what I had heard inside. He was too busy to say much, but I gathered that his men had been watching the mansion since the night before. They had sighted one of the burglars, and were now in pursuit of him across the opposite side of the park.

I must have ridden about a third of the way back when I was startled by something whizzing by me, and as it entered a patch of moonlight in front I saw a cyclist going at a tremendous pace, without a lamp. He was not one of the police, for I was just able to notice that he had no uniform. I at once thought of the burglar, and sprinted after him. I was faster than he, and as I put on the pace I soon caught sight of him again, and, despite his furious riding, began to overhaul him.

The road was tolerably straight, and unless he managed to dodge up a side turning I felt sure of him, as mine was clearly the swifter machine. Looking back in the light of calm reflection, I am by no means certain at the present time as to what would have happened had I managed to catch up to him. But I was too excited to think, and faster and faster the trees flew by as the distance between us shortened, until I could even catch the sound of laboured breathing as the humped figure in front of me ate up the miles that lay between him and safety.

Suddenly he gave a lurch to one side, and in the same breath seemed to collapse like an accordion. The whole thing was so instantaneous that at the rate I was travelling I was right on to him before I quite realised what had happened. With the inevitable collision uppermost in my mind, I instinctively wrenched at the handle-bar, mounted the bank at one side of the road, shot off again, and in another second had crashed into the opposite hedge, and was taking a header into the cornfield beyond.

By the time I had collected my wits, had scrambled to my feet, and hauled the cycle out of the hedge, I heard a murmur of voices and saw lights flitting about the road.

I crawled into it, and joined the police-sergeant and half a dozen of his men, excitedly gathered around the body of the fugitive. His fork-crown had given way, and although like a good rider he still grasped his handles, I saw at a glance by the unnatural twist of his neck that it was broken. As one of the men turned him over, and the light fell upon his face, we gave a simultaneous shout, for there, among the sparkling contents of a shattered jewel-case, lay Dr Ringmer!

Of course there was an inquest, and I was deputed by the coroner to make the post-mortem examination. My fees for the same I handed to Cave as a wedding gift, and as there was no chance of getting anything from Ringmer's representatives I had quite made up my mind to cycle back to town as poor as I arrived. But as I packed up I was handed a note enclosing a very handsome cheque, with some complimentary expressions. Both were signed, "Hepzibah Hammersmith."

Dr Ringmer was at once credited with the whole series of Crowham burglaries – whether justly or not I cannot say, but at any rate they abruptly ceased. With regard to the final one, my own theory is that he had planned it long beforehand, and (knowing the ducal failing) that my engagement and his own assumed illness were all part of an elaborate scheme, which but for a mere accident would have succeeded to admiration. The collection of "instruments" which had puzzled me so much is now, I believe, in the "Black Museum" at Scotland Yard.

# How I Attended a
# Nervous Patient

"And what do you think is the matter, Mrs Oakenfall?" I inquired.

"Well, really, sir, if it had been anyone else I should have said he'd got the horrors of drink on him. But then, Dr Cuthill knows there isn't a more temperate man in Borleywood."

"How long have you known him?"

"It'll be eighteen months come Michaelmas since he first came to live with me, and a quieter, nicer gentleman – for a foreigner – you couldn't wish to meet."

"What do you say he is?"

"A master at the college – teaches foreign languages, and suchlike. Eyetalian, they say he is, but you'd never know it from his manner, he's that polite; nor his speech either, though he don't always understand what I says to him."

"And he seems very strange?"

"*Scared*, doctor! Scared out of his senses! I was doing a bit of ironing in the afternoon, and was just thinking it was getting near Mr Valori's time for coming home, and he'd be wanting his tea presently, when all of a sudden he comes flying up the path and rushes into the house, overturning the ironing board, with never a by-your-leave, and him that's so civil always, and such a gentleman in his ways too.

"I see he was white as a corpse, with the sweat regular pouring off him, and he flew upstairs to his sitting-room and slammed the door and locked it for all the world as if the old gentleman was after him. It quite upset me for the time, but as soon as I'd put things straight again I went up and knocked at the door, and asked if he wanted anything. But he wouldn't give no answer, though I could hear him moving about; so I just came down and went a step or two down the garden path to see if I could see him at the window, but he'd got the blind drawn tight. I'm sure he must have seen me, though, for as soon as I looked up the blind gave a shake, just as if he'd been peeping round it like."

"Well, what next?" I suggested mildly, as Mrs Oakenfall paused and shook her head portentously. Cuthill had hinted, among other things, in his parting advice to me, that this was a person of some influence in the minor spheres of Borleywood. But she told her story with more than a trace of relish for its evident break in the monotony of her life, and as the morning was getting on I had other things beside her dignity to consider.

"Well, sir, I saw no more of him till the evening, when my daughter's husband came to bring me some eggs, for I use a good lot for omelettes and things for Mr Valori. I heard him unlatch his door and come creeping half-way down the stairs till he could see who it was talking to me. I went out and asked him if he wouldn't have anything to eat, but he called out, 'No, no, no!' and ran away back and shut himself in again.

"When I went up this morning and told him he *must* eat something he unlocked the door, and I could see he hadn't been to bed all night, and looked dreadfully peaky and ill. I gave him his breakfast, but it didn't seem as if he wanted any. He asked me to send word to the college that he wasn't well and shouldn't go out today, and I was to be sure and say he wasn't in if anyone came to see him. I asked him if I shouldn't send for the doctor, but he said, 'No,' but I don't think he meant it. As Dr Cuthill knows his constitution, I thought I'd ask him to give a look in, for I'm sure the poor gentleman ought to have some advice. Since you say Dr Cuthill's away, please don't let on to Mr Valori when you see him that I told you anything about him, will you, sir?"

"No, no; of course what you have told me is quite confidential. I shall be round presently."

I had been nearly a month at Burkfield, an engagement I had in a way secured for myself. Cuthill was – or perhaps it would be more correct to say his patients were – rather exacting as to the sort of man they expected him to leave in charge of his practice. He was somewhat averse to taking a stranger on the mere recommendation of an agent – even such a reliable one as my good friend Adamson. He was therefore not readily suited, and might have taken no holiday at all had he not heard of me through an old fellow-student – Walland, of Hampstead – at whose place I had that queer case of poisoning, already related, so it was now near the end of October.

St Martin's summer – if by calling it so I may anticipate the usual date of its arrival – is a season with very special charms for me, but never had it seemed so alluring as that day when I drove in the buggy to Borleywood. The road led over a series of undulating ridges, whose sandy surface, dry even with the late heavy rains, was withal so soft and springy that our course would have been noiseless but for the clashing of the cob's hoofs, the hind against the fore, an irritating vice he had lately contracted – his "castanet exercise," as I called it. All the way ran the heather, blazing in the autumn sun, a purple ribbon either side the road, and behind it again the odorous pines set a wall of deepest green to our horizon.

Presently we turned into the laurel-bordered drive of a great park, where rabbits shot every now and then across the way, and the lazy pheasants waddled in fancied security. Through a gate, and I once more inhaled deep breaths of the pungent air as a long, desolate-looking road opened before us, with a vista dim like a cathedral aisle as the arching branches met overhead. So thickly were the pine needles strewn that the squirrels were undisturbed by our approach, and I even caught a glimpse of white-shot wing and breast as a shy woodpecker darted into the further wood.

"A likely spot for a tragedy," I remarked to the groom, the thought suggested by the deadly gloom.

"Just so, sir," agreed Trevatt politely, although I doubt if the idea penetrated his Cornish stolidity.

The wildness of the place was indeed so depressing that I felt quite a sense of relief when we struck into a by-road which presently showed on the right. Leaving the wood behind us, we pulled up at the trimly-kept cottage on the outskirts of the dwellings around the college.

Mrs Oakenfall met me at the door.

"I told him you were coming," said she, "and I had a rare job to get him to stay in at first. But I think now he's rather glad, for he keeps on asking when you're coming."

In fear of more disclosures I merely nodded and followed the landlady upstairs. The room was so dark that as the door closed behind me I stood a moment endeavouring to get my bearings, but not a word came from the patient until, as I groped my way towards the window and raised the blind, a tremulous voice exclaimed, "It matters not!"

I turned in the direction of the speaker and saw a thin, dark-complexioned man crouching half-dressed upon the little iron bedstead. One trembling hand was plucking nervously at his beard, while with the other he motioned me to draw the blind again.

"I'm afraid I must have a little light upon you," I protested. "Is there anything the matter with your eyes?"

"No, no!" as he shrank still further away from the window.

I could see that he was in a half-hysterical condition, and hoping to gain time I began to talk of the college, and of the recent outbreak of measles there. After a while he ceased to answer in monosyllables, and as the nervous twitching of his hands decreased I managed to persuade him to lie down and let me overhaul him. There was very little the matter that I could discover except a good deal of palpitation, and as I gained his confidence he admitted that he had been overworked of late coaching pupils for an examination.

Nervous dyspepsia, thought I, and after a little more conversation I was about to leave him in a comparatively placid state when he startled me by bouncing off the bed, and before I could stop him had darted to the head of the stairs. He clung to the rails, listening intently, the rattle of a loose bannister voicing his nervous tremor the while.

His ears, more attentive than mine, had caught a knock at the cottage door, and it was not until apparently satisfied as to the identity of the milkman, whose conversation with Mrs Oakenfall I could now hear, that he relaxed his convulsive hold upon the rails and flung himself on the bed again.

"I was expecting someone from the college," was his explanation, delivered with an awkward smile. But I noticed that the sweat was standing in great drops upon his face, while the vessels of his neck pulsated fiercely.

"You must really take things more quietly," was my remonstrance – a lame one, no doubt, but the situation was embarrassing.

Promising to send him a tonic I groped downstairs, managing to elude Mrs Oakenfall on the way, and drove off more than a little puzzled. Alcoholism is certainly a many-sided affection, but terrifying as are the wild ideas of delirium tremens the schoolmaster's emotion I had seen to arise from actual occurrences. He was besides far too sensible in the intervals to give colour to any such diagnosis.

I was so intent on the matter that I paid no heed to someone hailing us, and had I been alone I should probably have driven on, but the stopping of the cart woke me to a sense of my responsibilities.

Trevatt had pulled up at a farmhouse I had noticed several times in my rounds, never failing to admire the charming picture it made, regrettable as was the main cause. I learned at one time and another that it had been the homestead of a large farming estate which had fallen upon evil days, much of the land having been merged in neighbouring farms while the house remained a melancholy derelict. It was in the red-brick and timber style so common thereabouts, but ruin had clothed it with a special grace, and the ivy that crept unrestrained to the very roof softened the ravages of weather and neglect.

Deserted for many a year, it had lately been hired by an artist who was content to overlook its discomfort for the sake of its picturesque appearance. Its cheapness had perhaps not a little to do with his selection. This was the man who stood, a black-bearded figure, at an open lower window.

"Please come in, doctor. I've hurt my foot."

The low-ceiled room I entered, its blackened beams fairly bristling with hooks, had evidently been the kitchen and living-room of the farm. The huge cavern of a fireplace along one side was still furnished with broad oak settles, cosy enough no doubt when the fire blazed on the hearth and the wind whistled outside. But now there was a sense of musty dampness about the place, and the small windows with their little diamond-panes gave exceedingly little light for an artist's studio. For that it was indeed the studio was evidenced by the trade-marks of the craft all about; but this I will say, it was the neatest studio I have ever seen.

"Sorry to trouble you," said the artist as he hobbled across the room, leaning heavily on a stick. Sliding on to a ricketty old sofa, he drew off his sock and showed me one of the worst sprains I had ever seen or am likely to see. As I examined it carefully, to make sure there was no fracture, he explained how he had been sauntering through a dark avenue the day before, and had slipped on some wet leaves.

"Do you mean that long drive just at the end of the road?" I asked. "It would make a good background for a tragic composition, don't you think?"

"Yes, yes, yes!" he exclaimed, starting, and half rising; adding, with a groan as the sprain reminded him of his crippled condition, "very tragic, as you say."

"You are no Englishman," I thought as he spoke, so soft was the inflection of his voice, the gestures so forceful and animated.

"Excuse me," I said aloud. "What is your name?"

"Smithson," was the dogged reply, and I straightway entered it in my visiting list, but I was unconvinced. The eyes, now that I scanned him closely, were too liquid, and that lustrous black hair and olive complexion were never owned by a pure-blooded Smith or Smithson either.

Now, I am not an artist, but I had smoked too many pipes in my friend Havery's studio not to have assimilated a little of the jargon. As I took a roll of tape-strapping from my bag and proceeded to truss up the ankle, I turned the conversation into what I imagined was a congenial topic. But he either resented my talking shop, or else the pain of the ankle made him irritable. Anyhow, he was clearly uncomfortable, especially when I ventured a joke on the extraordinary cleanliness of his brushes, which stood in a tall jar on the mantelpiece as rustless a sheaf as if they had just left the makers.

As I rose and stretched myself after bending over the ankle I took care to make no similar remark as to a spotless palette hanging opposite me. It seemed every whit as clean as the brushes, and bore none of that peculiar gloss which follows repeated washings of paint. But although determined to be careful what I said, I nevertheless had a good look around the room.

It struck me as an odd thing that a stock of unused canvases should be all of one size. Was he, I thought, a manufacturer of pot-boilers by the square foot? I turned to half a dozen finished pictures standing round the walls, and noted that they were all landscapes. Curiously enough, every one of them was in a totally different style.

"Your own work?" I queried.

"Yes!" came the abrupt answer. Smithson, without being exactly a genius, was certainly a very versatile painter. For instance, I never saw so many ways of treating skies from the same hand. The odd thing was that a sea-piece which really might have passed for an unknown work of Stanfield's stood next to a positive atrocity, which the conductor of a cheap illustrated paper would have hesitated to foist upon the public at Christmas time. Indeed, it was the very outrageousness of the latter which threw the particular merit of its neighbour into such prominence, and led me to the most astonishing discovery I made in this truly astonishing studio.

It arose in this way. Some two or three weeks before I came down to Borleywood, after paying a visit to Adamson, the medical agent, and returning along the Strand with nothing in particular to do, I ran against Havery, similarly situated. We presently stopped outside a picture-dealer's, where Havery must needs illustrate his usual growl at the crassness of the public taste by the lamentable exhibition of "art" in the window. He was good enough to omit one picture from his censure, and taking it in detail point by point, expiated on the merits of open-air work and the "Newlyn stroke," to which he carefully drew my attention. All this came back to me as I gazed, for there, staring me in the face, was the self-same canvas, "Newlyn stroke" and all!

Havery had identified the signature – that of a quite unknown man, but destined, he said, for great things in the future if he survived so long – and I searched eagerly for it in the corner. As I might have expected, it had disappeared, but its former position was clearly shown where it had been daubed over with a splash of "art enamel." And, as I lived, the same clumsy trick had been played upon every one of the pictures I was near enough to inspect.

"You like that?"

I started at the question, managed to blurt out, "Oh, very much – very nice indeed!" and sat down without knowing what to do or say next.

I think I made some irrelevant remark in a desperate attempt to regain my composure, but all that I remember with any clearness is that the conversation, which was really a monologue on the artist's part, somehow drifted round to foreign travel, and for the first time he appeared to be entirely at his ease.

This mood was a very passing one, however. He was talking of the South of France, Switzerland, and then Italy, when I interjected a remark about Sassoferrato. Instantly his manner changed. He was obviously perturbed, and the fluent speech became a stutter tinged at once with that unmistakable foreign accent. One would have thought he had never heard the name before. And Sassoferrato, too, whose pictures are to be found in nearly every church and gallery in Italy! The situation was really too absurd.

As I rose to go, I question which of us was the more embarrassed; but as for myself, I am certain that a more awkward exit was never made by a novice in the art of leaving a patient.

"Have I been long?" I asked Trevatt as we drove away.

"Not so very long, sir," was the diplomatic reply, deftly flicking the cob on the neck as the latter resumed his castanet exercise.

Two new patients, and each a greater mystery than the other, I reflected.

The next day, and daily for a week, I visited the schoolmaster, and either because of my treatment or in spite of it he rapidly mended, regaining the calm suavity of manner his lapse from which Mrs Oakenfall had so lamented. It was a queer attack, truly, and at times I felt tempted to dismiss it as a case of alcoholism pure and simple, but for one thing.

I discovered very soon that he had a disease of the heart which, although not accounting for all the symptoms, went a long way to explain some of them. I certainly had not discovered it when I first saw him, and it is possible that his nervous tremors prevented me hearing accurately at the time. At any rate, the affection was plain enough now, being of that variety which has been attributed to nervous shock or strain, and therein it tallied with Mrs Oakenfall's account of the onset of his illness.

At the end of a week he had so far recovered as to sit out in the little quaint old-fashioned garden at the back of the cottage, well planted with hollyhocks, showing little of their short-lived summer gorgeousness. I found he was fond of cycling, and as the roads thereabouts were fairly level I consented to his taking a daily potter awheel, and put him on the "occasional" column of my visiting list.

All this time I had not been neglecting Smithson, who also prospered under my hands. I must confess that, quite apart from the uninteresting nature of his complaint, and although there was nothing repellent about the man, I never felt quite at ease in his company. It would have been quite impossible for me to give any logical reason for this, but it might perhaps have arisen from a vague sense of irritation at the mystery which seemed to enshroud his occupation. Although I had called at all sorts of hours, arranging the visit so as to suit the rest of my round, I never found him at work. What seemed more puzzling, I was never able to detect the least sign of his doing any. The pile of new canvases lay as undisturbed, the brushes and palette as cleanly, as on my first visit.

He appeared to spend all his time reading yellow paper-covered French novels. He was certainly always ready for a talk, but here again he studiously avoided any hint of art matters. The only topic which seemed to interest him was foreign politics and travel, on which I need hardly say he did most of the talking. Very excellent talking it was, too, for he was a man of education, possessed of great natural shrewdness, cosmopolitan in the best sense of the word. Had I been about to start practice on the Riviera, for instance, the information he imparted would have been invaluable. So far as I could see he had no visitors, nor had he any servants, being looked after by an old dame from the village. He was so much of a recluse that I had some difficulty in persuading him, as his ankle grew stronger, to sit and read in the open air.

It was about a fortnight after my first meeting with Smithson that the incident occurred which converted the feeling of distrust I entertained for him to one of positive aversion. I had been called to a farm just beyond Borleywood in the middle of breakfast, when, Trevatt being busy, I took my cycle. On the way back I thought I would look in upon Valori. I found him out – riding, Mrs Oakenfall said. She added that he had picked up wonderfully, and seemed to have quite regained his spirits.

As I rode homewards the long avenue looked more ghost-haunted than usual, and I was glad to turn out of it and enjoy the free-wheeling afforded by the switchback road leading straight into Burkfield. Before me stretched the heather-bordered track, and presently the wind sang in my ears with the swift rush down, up, and down again over the rolling sandy ridges.

Exhilarated with the motion and by the resinous breath of the pines, so light-hearted did I feel that I could have even forgiven Smithson some of his peculiarities. Nearing the derelict farm, I was half inclined to call and wipe off a visit – perhaps the final one, as he was now practically well again.

Just as I had decided to do this I topped the last ridge before the long, level Burkfield Road, and for the first time saw that I was not alone upon it. Another cyclist had just completed the switchback, and as I overhauled him I recognised Valori, pedalling gently in the same direction. The schoolmaster appeared delighted to see me, and I remembered afterwards how cheery was his manner, and what a colour glowed in his cheeks from the exercise.

"You are not out for pleasure, doctor?"

"No, indeed. I have only had half a breakfast; just got back from one visit and I'm thinking of making another over there." I pointed to the farm just ahead.

He made the stock remark of a man who had never known what it is not to be able to take a meal in peace nor to go to bed devoutly praying that he may be allowed at least four hours of unbroken peace:

"I should not like to be a doctor."

"A dog's life; only a degree less miserable than that of a sailor," was my stock rejoinder.

"Is anyone living at the farm there?" he inquired after a pause.

"Oh, yes! An artist. By the by, he's a great traveller and knows the Continent well. You might like to make his acquaintance. There he is, by Jove!"

I had just caught sight of Smithson sitting at the door with a book (the inevitable French novel, I suppose) in his hand. Although we were talking naturally our approach must have been fairly silent, for even as I spoke Smithson looked up with a start, as if only just aware of us.

I had risen on the pedal to dismount, and was just about to call "Good morning" to him, when there was a loud crash behind me. Craning my neck, I saw poor Valori lying in a heap, with his cycle fallen in the ditch. I was beside him in a second, and so deathly pale did he look, that at first I was inclined to think the heart trouble had asserted itself and that he was quite dead. But he still breathed, and dragging him to one side, I called to Smithson to bring some water.

I waited a minute or two, and then, as no reply came, ran up the three or four steps into the little front garden, only to find it deserted. There was the chair, certainly, with a book and pipe lying beside it; indeed, but for this evidence I might have imagined that my vision of Smithson had been an optical illusion.

Almost equally annoyed as amazed, I walked to the door and tried it. It was fast locked! Now, I was determined that Smithson should not fool me in this way, so I alternately kicked at the door, and kept up such a din against it with my fists, shouting the while, that none but a person of stony deafness could have failed to hear me. The door, which by reason of its age was none of the strongest, began to show signs of yielding to my onslaught, when the Levite apparently gave way to the Samaritan, and Smithson appeared on the threshold with a jug in his hand.

He offered it to me with the cool inquiry, "Do you want some water, doctor?" I could have flung it in his face, but swallowing the speech that was on the tip of my tongue I took it in silence.

Valori had not regained consciousness, and although I held nitrate of amyl to his nostrils, the slight pulse was scarcely improved. I was turning back to insist on Smithson giving him temporary shelter when the jog-trot of an approaching cart sounded very musically to me. It was the Borleywood carrier, one Leathersole, who pulled up on seeing the state of affairs. Between us we laid poor Valori in the bottom of the cart, and storing the two machines inside, set out to return.

All the time there was no further sign of Smithson, although I could feel that he was watching me from behind the closed window. On the way to Borleywood I continued my treatment, which I was relieved to find successful just before we arrived there.

After seeing Valori safely to bed, I made a second start for Burkfield – and breakfast.

The morning having been so muddled, I was running after time all the rest of the day, and it was not until the early evening that I was able to work round to Borleywood.

Valori, I learned, had been very restless. He was constantly calling for assistance, and whenever Mrs Oakenfall obeyed the summons she found him as nervous as in his previous attack. As I went upstairs all seemed quiet, and I thought I could hear the sound of regular breathing, as if Valori were asleep. But just as I got to the door there was an agonised scream, followed by words, which, although in a tongue to me unknown, were the accents of unmitigated horror and apprehension. Rushing in, I found him sitting up in bed with an expression of the most abject terror I have ever seen on a man's face.

"Come, come, Mr Valori! There's nothing to be nervous at," I exclaimed soothingly. But the nearer I drew, the further away he cowered and motioned me off with a tremulous hand as if still haunted by the spectre of his dream.

"Why, don't you know me? Don't you remember our ride together this morning?" I marvelled that the accident had so upset him, and almost feared that I had overlooked some injury to his head which was causing delirium.

"What happened to me? What did you do to me?" he demanded with a positive scowl.

"Happened?" I repeated, with an attempt at a hearty laugh. "Why, I think you must have overdone the cycling and fainted. Anyhow, you parted company with the machine, and were such a long time coming to that I don't know what I should have done if Leathersole the carrier hadn't come along and given us a lift."

"Why did you take me to that house?"

"I took you to no house; you fainted before we got there."

"Who is it lives there?"

"A Mr Smithson, an artist."

"Why did he tell you to bring me?"

"He never did so. I never mentioned you to him. He has travelled in your country and knows it well, and I thought if I introduced you, you might be glad to know each other."

"Is he a friend of yours?"

"He is a patient."

"How long have you known him?"

"About as long as I have known you. But – "

"What is the matter?" he interrupted. "Why do you go there?"

This was a little too much for me. I had already been catechised to an extent I would have endured from no one else, and I felt unable to humour him any longer.

"Really, Signor Valori," I protested, "I cannot discuss my patients with you or anyone else."

"Enough – enough!" And lying down again he turned his back to me.

Ungracious, even suspicious as was his manner, he was clearly not delirious, and hoping that a sound sleep would tranquillise him, I filled a medicine glass from the sedative I had brought with me and offered it to him.

The next instant it was spanked from my hand to the other side of the room, with the vicious exclamation, *"Ladrone!* You shall not poison me!"

As I picked up the glass he crouched into bed again, and burying himself beneath the clothes, obstinately refused to stir or utter another word. I could do no more. The conviction was gradually shaping itself that he was a lunatic, and warning Mrs Oakenfall to watch him discreetly, as any excitement might easily prove fatal, and above all not to irritate him by unnecessary attentions, I left.

Other work, already in arrears, prevented me from giving much thought to Valori for the rest of the evening. I rose next morning with the idea of sending to London for a male attendant, a determination which was strengthened by an urgent message from Borleywood arriving before I was well dressed.

By the time I had swallowed a few mouthfuls of breakfast Trevatt was ready for me. My idea was to send him on to the post office at Borleywood with a wire for the attendant while I was seeing Valori, and as we drove along I scrawled the message on my knee. It was no easy task to write in a jolting dog-cart, and I was touching up some of the more tremulous letters when Trevatt pulled up with a jerk.

"Mr Smithson, sir," was his exclamation; and sure enough it was the artist, who approached, calm and unconcerned as ever.

"Good morning, doctor. If you are going to Borleywood, do you mind giving me a lift? My ankle isn't very strong just yet, and I want to sketch a farm out that way."

My opinion of Smithson being what it was, I should have ignored him had I been alone. But Trevatt knew so much of other people's affairs that I rather suspected him of being a gossip, and was anxious accordingly that he should not see any lack of cordiality on my part.

For the same reason I was unable to tell Smithson as I should like to have done what I thought of his behaviour as regards Valori. As graciously as I could, then, I invited him to get up behind, and for the sake of appearances exchanged a few commonplace remarks during the short drive. But I felt uncomfortable. Even now I was sure Smithson was lying to me, for he had neither sketch-book, colour-box, nor any of the other paraphernalia of the painting artist. It was strange how vividly he always managed to convey the impression that he had something to conceal.

Arrived at the cottage, I sent Trevatt off with the telegram, and was taking a very formal farewell of my passenger when a voice screamed, "Doctor! Quick! He's dying!" It was Mrs Oakenfall, intensely excited.

I flew up the red-tiled path, but, seizing my arm, she dragged me from the stairs as I had got my foot upon the first step.

"This way – in the garden!" she cried.

At the bottom of the garden, fully-dressed and clutching a hand-bag, the Italian lay prone against the fence which bordered the little plot of grass and flowers. As I raised him I caught a faint whisper of *"Mafiosi!"* Presently I felt the last flicker of his pulse as there faded in his eyes the ghastly, horrified expression, witness of his haunting terrors to the last.

"Ah, poor gentleman!" Mrs Oakenfall sobbed. "He never stayed in bed after you left yesterday. His boxes are all turned out, and he must have been sorting them over and over all night. I didn't disturb him, as you told me not, 'cept to bring his breakfast. But he wouldn't open the door, and I took it away. I never went near him again till I see you coming, sir, and then I went up. He'd got the door open then, and was ready dressed with his coat and hat on, when I said, 'Here's the doctor,' he went to the window, and before I could stir he'd snatched up the bag and was down the stairs two at a time. He tried to get into the field there, for when I got out he was kind of struggling to get his leg over the fence, and then he gave such a groan and fell down here."

"Is he dead?"

I turned and saw Smithson. He must have followed me through the house. For answer I closed the dead man's eyes. Smithson laughed hysterically. I faced him, all my pent-up resentment bursting out.

"This is a private house, Mr Smithson, and let me tell you that your presence here is an intrusion. But since you have sneaked in behind me, I'll tell you that the more I see of you the less I like you, and I consider that you acted in a mean and cowardly manner when this poor fellow was in need of assistance the other day."

I clenched my fist in readiness for the blow which I quite expected would have answered me, and felt thankful that Mrs Oakenfall, in search of help, would be no witness to an undignified scuffle in her back-garden. But Smithson had either less self-respect or more self-restraint than I anticipated.

"I admit," said he, "that I have given you cause to say all that you have – and more! As I am shortly leaving here I will take this opportunity of thanking you for your attention to myself, for which I will send you the fee at once." He raised his hat to me, and before, in my astonishment, I had thought of something to say in reply, had disappeared.

Had I been more ready-witted with Smithson in the garden he would still have had the last word, for when I came down to breakfast a couple of mornings after I found a letter waiting me, endorsed, "With Mr Smithson's compliments and thanks." It bore the London post-mark, and contained a ten-pound note (at least twice as much as Cuthill would have expected for the attendance), and the following remarkable statement:

"When you receive this I shall have left England for ever. My real name is immaterial to you, but I am not the least among a brotherhood more powerful than kings and emperors, numberless as the motes in a sunbeam, widely diffused as its light. Some two years ago a member violated its laws, and was adjudged to die by his own hand. The coward fled, and another man was selected to execute his sentence. That traitor you knew as Valori, the avenger was myself. We were both chemists by profession, and he had betrayed for gain the secret of a new and deadly explosive invented by me. I tracked him to his hiding-place, met him in the lonely avenue, and would have killed him but for the accident in pursuing him which introduced me to you. My mission has not been unsuccessful. Think more kindly of me. Adieu."

From the last word of the dying Valori I imagined the brotherhood alluded to by "Smithson" was the Mafia, the infamous society which to this day practically though secretly governs Sicily and much of Italy as well.

It only remains for me to add that the most remarkable thing about this remarkable communication was its fate in my possession. In packing up to leave Burkfield about a week later, I found the envelope intact. But although the letter was safe inside, the paper was an absolute blank! It must have been written upon with vanishing ink, a composition known to every analytical chemist.

# How I Met a Very Ignorant Practitioner

"So you're Dr Wilkinson," said Dr Inns. "Rather young, an't you? I've never had a local what-d'you-call-it before, but anyone from Adamson's sure to be all right. Been expecting you all day. Come in."

Adamson, the agent, good fellow that he was, never left me long unemployed, so here I was at Hestford – Hestford-on-the-Wash, about the last place that was created, I should say. As I cycled the couple of miles from the station, leaving my traps to follow, I wondered what on earth could have induced any man to settle in such an out-of-the-way corner. The country was flat and sparsely wooded, and the Virginia creeper, which covered the little house with just a trace of autumn bronzing, was about the only dash of colour in a singularly grey and cheerless landscape.

Dr Inns, as he called himself, and as I shall therefore call him, was squat and thickset, with a mop of red hair and a stiff beard that looked as if he had forgotten to shave for a week, so short and stubby was it. He was active enough for all his stoutness, and as I followed him through the cottage – it was nothing more – I noticed he was full of funny little jerks and starts, peering about him in bird-fashion as if he feared an assailant at every turn. He opened the door of a room which I took to be the parlour, and curling up in the only easy chair, left me to find a seat for myself.

"We'd better get to business," said he, "as I leave early tomorrow. Now this here's the room where I see everybody who comes – the consulting room you'd call it – eh?"

I murmured something in reply, and cast a wondering look round. I have never seen a consulting room that so successfully concealed its character as this, for the only thing professional about the place was a battered old wooden stethoscope up on the mantel. Inns was evidently a practititioner of the old school, who scorned new-fangled aids to diagnosis. I am afraid I was taking too much stock of the room to pay heed to what he said. He must have been talking for some time, but I fortunately began to listen just at the right moment.

"And now to tell you about this here case," he was saying. "He's had this inflammation of the lungs on him for the last six months."

"Six months!" I exclaimed in astonishment at such a record.

"Ah! All that and more," with a sage shake of the head.

"Is the temperature still high?"

"It's never been high."

My jaw fell.

"What! With pneumonia?" I protested.

"He's not had nemonia." This very doggedly. "I said, inflammation of the lungs."

This was a facer, and as it was the first time I had ever heard that the popular and scientific terms were not indicative of the same disease, I could find nothing to say and patiently awaited a further access of information.

"Well, that's all about Ikin."

"What is the patient?" I ventured to ask.

"Oh, he's a miller – worth every penny of forty thousand pounds. He's been getting rather fidgetty lately; talked of having a consultation. But there's no other doctor anywhere nearer than Treacham, and I ain't on speaking terms with the man there. The only other one who's bad is Warkwell, the old wharfinger. He's got St Anthony's fire."

"Heavens!" I thought. "If that is how he speaks of erysipelas I shall expect to hear of 'jail fever' and the 'sweating sickness' next!"

"Do you make up your own medicines?" I asked when I had recovered sufficiently.

"Rather! There's no chemist nearer than Treacham. I've got an A-1 little surgery, I can tell you. Just come and have a look at it."

He got up and opened a door opposite the one we had entered by. Within was a long, cupboard-like place, rather dark in spite of its white-washed walls. But after all I had seen hitherto I was quite unprepared for what was in store for me. I expected to find just a mere handful of drugs, but, as a matter of fact, the array of bottles and jars, tier on tier, bright with gilt-lettering, from floor to ceiling, would have been no discredit to a London chemist's shop. As I turned round to thoroughly inspect the place I caught Dr Inns' eye.

"Ah, I thought it'd fetch you! All done from London; gave 'em a blank manifest when I first came down here."

One thing that struck me was the enormous stock of everything he seemed to keep; not a bottle that was not full to the stopper. But when, attracted by some very fine crystals, I took one down for closer inspection, I found that it was not only thickly coated with dust, but the stopper was so firmly fixed that I doubt if it had ever been opened since it was put there! Inns had been watching me, and I noticed that he looked as awkward as I felt, so I put the bottle on the shelf again. Casting about for some topic to break the silence, my eye fell on what I concluded was his day-book.

"Oh, is this the day-book?" I asked.

"Yes, that's it," and he opened the parchment bound volume and ran a coarse and rather dirty finger down the pages.

Now I have seen some curious day-books, both before and since then, but I think this was about the most curious of all. Here were none of the cabalistic signs and jargon which have such a puzzling effect upon the uninitiated. The weights and quantities were written at full length – "ounces," "drachms," "grains," etc.; the drugs, too, were set down in their conventional English names, while the directions appeared in the homeliest vernacular. In a word, the entries had very much the appearance of those in some housewife's book of recipes. So, far from no one but himself being able to understand Dr Inns' day-book – not at all an unusual occurrence in the case of a busy practitioner – I think it would have appeared quite simple to even non-professional readers.

"Know this here?" he asked, reaching up to a shelf above the desk, and taking down a fat volume, which he held out to me. I looked at it; it was a *Popular Physician*.

"First-rate book," he commented as he turned over the leaves, which I could see were thumbed and dog's-eared with long service.

"First-rate, as you say," I agreed. At the same time I wondered what occult reason could induce any medical man to constitute half his library of reference from an elementary work intended solely for the unprofessional public. I say "half his library," for this and one other book were all that I could see in the place, the second volume being *The Shipmaster's Medical Guide,* a work which the Board of Trade regulations require every ship not provided with a surgeon of its own to carry as a guide to the medicine chest.

Looking at it, I was reminded of the story of the captain who, finding that a sailor's symptoms required the aid of a mixture of which he was short – say, No. 9 – made up the required medicine by half a dose of No. 5, and a similar quantity of No. 4, to the entire satisfaction of all concerned.

Altogether Dr Inns was a curious study, and when we had presently discussed a meal, which being neither a late dinner nor an early supper was a mixture of both, I spent a very amusing evening listening to his yarns of sea-life, for it presently came out that he had spent several years in the "South American Steam Navigation Company's" service.

For some reason which he did not disclose, he appeared to have grown restless and dissatisfied with his present lot. As the evening wore on he grew so far communicative as to tell me that his absence would not be all holiday-making.

"I'm going up to London to see if Adamson can't sell this practice," said he.

"Going to sea again?" I suggested.

"Well, no; not exactly. Don't know what I shall do when I clear out. Do nothing for a little while, p'raps. Not that I'm overworked here. You'll have nothing to do but these two visits, so far as I know."

"You're wanting me for a fortnight, aren't you?" I replied.

"Well, yes, I think so. I may take a run over to Paris for a day or two while Adamson is finding someone to buy the practice. If you need to know anything, just write to me, 'care of Adamson,' but I don't expect I shall be far away."

As he remarked, he certainly did not seem to be overworked. From the time I arrived in the late afternoon until we went to bed about eleven, no patients put in an appearance. Like the rest of the house, my bedroom was furnished with a Spartan simplicity which I put down to Inns' pronounced nautical tastes. But I liked it all the better for that, and turning in, I slept soundly until awakened in the morning by Inns himself.

He told me not to hurry down to breakfast, as he had to catch an early train. The little pony-cart in which he did his rounds was already waiting, and he drove away after bidding me farewell in the unconventional style which marked all his actions. The same elderly woman who had waited on us in the evening gave me breakfast, and with the groom, or page (his were composite duties, as I found), seemed to make up the entire establishment.

I dawdled over breakfast, for there seemed little else to fill up the time with, and a newspaper was unheard of in such a place. The trap returned by the time I had finished, but I sent out word that I preferred to cycle rather than drive, and after a smoke I sallied out to pay my two visits.

I found the miller in his house on one side of the square formed by the mill and a long stretch of granaries. He lay on a sofa by an open window, from which he was able to superintend the unloading of some grain. He looked hale and hearty enough, and greeted me with a cordiality which scarcely surprised me when I remembered his wish to have a "second opinion."

"And how do you find yourself today, Mr Ikin?" I asked after listening to the long history of his troubles.

"Oh, I'm in the same miserable condition," he said with an air of profound self-pity.

"No better?"

"Not a bit!"

"But you've got no cough now," I urged.

"Never had one."

I gasped. And he had had inflammation of the lungs, too.

"Dr Inns tells me you had no particular fever."

"No. He used to take my temperature at first, but the thermometer never showed anything, however long I sat on it. There it is; would you like to try it?" He pointed to an ordinary household thermometer (the shilling kind, made in Germany) that hung on the wall!

It was lucky he did so, for in another second I should have given Inns away by producing my own neat little "thirty second" clinical thermometer from my waistcoat.

Honestly, I would have given a sovereign at that moment to be able to laugh. At the risk of apoplexy, I managed to control the emotion, but I am sure I must have turned purple with the effort. If only the miller would have made a joke, even the feeblest, so that I could have had an excuse to explode comfortably! But he was dismally serious, so to save the situation I insisted on thoroughly overhauling him, finding nothing amiss but dyspepsia and a general flabbiness, the result of want of exercise. By the time I had finished the more acute spasms of my hilarity were vanquished, and assuring him that his lungs were quite sound, I ventured no opinion as to what their former condition might have been.

As he was taking no medicine, having refused further dosing in disgust, there was no treatment for me to alter. I did the best I could by strictly enjoining his wife to attend to his diet, and to send him out for a daily walk.

On the whole, I got over the interview better than I could have expected, but never prisoner enjoyed his freedom more heartily than did I as I rode from the house, wobbling dangerously with pent-up mirth. Indeed, as soon as I had safely turned a corner of the road, I was forced to tumble off the machine and, sitting on a bank, laughed till the tears cascaded down my cheeks.

After such an experience I had a curious anxiety about the next patient. I looked him up in my visiting list. "Warkwell, wharf labourer, erysipelas." Inns, truly, called it "St Anthony's fire," but this had been too unscientific for me, although it was clear that diagnosis was not his strong point. I doubted if he could have gone far wrong in such a case.

I had been directed none too clearly to the place, and must have gone altogether astray, for after inquiring the road several times I seemed to be moving in a circle. I arrived at the house at dinner-time, to judge by the smell that reminded me how long ago I had breakfasted. The whole family, including the patient, were enjoying a leg of salt pork – hardly the most suitable diet for erysipelas.

My first impulse was to retire, with an apology for interrupting the meal, but this was so warmly opposed that I stayed on. I was not very much surprised to see no evidence of erysipelas either present or recent; it was only what I expected. But I did wonder how Inns had failed to see that the man was really suffering from scurvy. I recognised it as such at the first glance; indeed, I never met with a more typical case.

"It's main catchin', this," observed Warkwell. "We've all had it, but somehow it's sarved me worser'n any."

"Perhaps you eat a good deal of pork?" I ventured.

"Yes. I gets it cheap from the shippin' stores."

"I think you'd be better without it."

"Why, Dr Inns takes it an' thrives on it. I've heard him say theer's nothin' like it."

I felt conscientiously indignant at this, and straightway attacked his pork dietary, telling him he would never get well until he took fresh meat, with plenty of vegetables, and especially lemon, or at least home-made lemonade. But I could see that neither Warkwell nor his wife believed me, and fearing they might construe my advice into an attack upon Inns, I rode away home in a much less cheerful frame of mind than when I arrived.

It was impossible, I thought, to regard Inns as anything else than an incompetent ass, yet he was well qualified, and had a fair record in the *Medical Directory*. It was a good thing his practice was small, or Heaven help Hestford! And then I began to wonder if his incompetence was getting known, and whether that might not be the reason for his wanting to clear out while he still had any practice left to dispose of. Anyhow, I determined to let him know on the first opportunity what I thought of Warkwell's case, for I felt I should otherwise be an accessory to the practical murder of the poor creature.

Towards the end of the fortnight, I seized what looked like a last opportunity of cycling across country to the cathedral town, and was pumping up my tyres after dinner when I was told that "the doctor's mother and sister" had called to see him and would like to speak with me.

Wondering what they could possibly want, I obeyed the summons, and found them sitting in the parlour consulting-room. The mother was an aristocratic-looking old dame, with that kind of silvery hair which always looks as if it had been powdered in the fashion of long ago, its striking effect being heightened by a pair of very piercing black eyes. The daughter, barring the white hair, was a replica of her mother, and, I should say, if anything, more handsome and elegant than she had ever been. Altogether, greater contrast to the son and brother it would be difficult to imagine.

The old lady received my explanations with a stately grace through which I thought I could detect more than a shadow of annoyance.

"Did my son leave no message for me when he went away?" she inquired.

"None whatever that I am aware of. But perhaps the housekeeper – "

"My son would leave no message with a servant!" she interrupted, and went on. "It is really very strange. I wrote and said we should be here today."

"Have you come far?"

"From London," rather shortly; and then resumed her catechism. "Has Dr *Inns* been gone long?"

"Nearly a fortnight. I expect him back in a day or two."

"Did he say where he was going?"

"To London, I think."

"Did he leave you no address, then?"

"Only that of the agent through whom he engaged me."

Her ladyship looked supercilious.

"I am very much obliged to you," she said rising. "I will come again as soon as Dr Inns returns."

I should have liked much to lengthen the interview. The daughter had never said a word the whole time, and I was anxious to hear her voice. Meanwhile, she had been looking round the room, and whenever her eyes met mine they regarded me as unconcernedly as if I were part of the furniture – a mere chattel of the place. Such eyes as they were, too! Deep and liquid, with none of her mother's keenness about them.

I was young and susceptible in those days. But as I could think of nothing to detain them longer, I could only rise with the best grace I could muster, and as I showed them to the door the silent maiden so far condescended as to return my bow with a half smile. After all, it is not in woman to resent homage, even if it is unspoken. And I must have disclosed the admiration I felt for her as plainly as if I had fallen on my knees to humbly avow it.

The next morning brought a letter from Inns. He was anxious to know how the patients were going on – at least he said so, but seeing how little he appeared to trouble about them when at home I was sceptical as to his interest in them when away. The letter was very brief – only half a dozen lines or so; and he addressed it from Adamson's office. The housekeeper was clearing the breakfast table as I read it, and apologetically asked me for any news of Inns.

"Well, really, Mrs Walsham, the doctor says nothing about himself, and only asked me about the patients."

"Ah, he'll be sorry to hear his dear mother and sister have been again. It seems so misfortunate 'tis always so."

"Why, have they missed each other before?" I never encourage servants to talk, but for once my curiosity got the better of my judgement.

"Time and again, sir, have they been; but the doctor he's always away from home at the time."

"Do you mean to say they never meet?"

"Not to my knowledge, sir. I've been with the doctor all the time he's lived in Hestford – and that's two year come next Michaelmas – and never yet have they found him. I thought maybe he'd gone up to Lon'on to see them."

A curious state of things, truly, I thought. The situation was even farcical, if farce could possibly be associated with such a haughty pair as the lady and her daughter. I hesitated whether I should say anything about them in my reply. I had an opinion, and a very decided one, as to the two patients, but that I shrank from giving Inns at present, and certainly not in writing. But if I avoided the subject, I really should have nothing to say to him. In the end I alluded to the patients with a vague optimism, and filled up the letter with an account of his visitors, adding that they hoped to see him on his return.

Inns must have been in close attendance at Adamson's, for he sent a reply practically by return of post. He was very busy, negotiations for sale in active progress, only a small sum dividing him from a possible purchaser, quite impossible to return, and so on. The gist of it all, could I wait another week? As I had nothing else in view, and one berth was as good as another, I wrote and consented to stay on.

I had just sent the boy off to the post when Mrs Walsham told me a gentleman, she thought a new patient, was asking for the doctor. She introduced a tall man, with features of a rather foreign cast, but refined and intellectual withal. He seemed much tanned by exposure, and the lower part of his face was practically hidden by a close black beard. There was an odd reminder about him of someone else – just whom I was unable at the moment to decide.

"Dr Inns?" he inquired, as he sat down, adding, when I had explained matters, "Ah! I thought there must be some mistake, although it's a good many years since I saw him."

"Did you wish to see him professionally?"

"Oh, no, thanks. I knew him in the South American line, and, being in the neighbourhood, I thought I would look him up. Is he as stout as ever?"

"Well, I never met him till a few days ago, but he is certainly rather stout."

"Does he grow his beard now? We were always chaffing him about the way he used to cut himself in shaving, and he used to tell a yarn, I remember, about the number of razors he blunted."

"Yes," I said, "he grows his beard. As to yarns, he has the finest assortment I ever heard."

"Ah, a thorough good fellow. When do you expect him back?"

"In a week for certain, I should say. Who shall I tell him called?"

"Oh, never mind, I want to surprise him. He always enjoyed a practical joke. I can easily run over, as I'm staying at Treacham for the present."

The stranger hardly looked the sort of man one would expect to indulge in practical jokes, and when he had taken his leave I could not help wondering how a man of such obvious refinement could have any serious liking for one of the stamp of Inns, although no doubt the monotony of shipboard has accounted for queerer friendships. For my own part, I could have wished his stay longer, so much was I beginning to feel the dead-and-aliveness of the place.

Ever since our meeting I had been thinking pretty constantly of Inns' sister, and as the third week progressed I told myself each morning that that day I should see her. Shall I confess it? The idea had weighed more than a little with me when I agreed to stay on the extra week. Each day I rose hopefully, and each night I went to bed and lay awake inventing all kinds of reasons for my disappointment. They might be weeks perhaps before they came back; or if they came they might just inquire at the door if Inns had returned and go away again. Or worse still, Mrs Inns might come alone. All this I told myself, and in the telling I wished I had a month longer to stay, but the last day came round so quickly that the week seemed as if it had been half its proper length.

Inns was delightfully vague in all his arrangements, and I was quite in the dark as to what time of the day he would return. As it was no good leaving things till the last moment, I spent a depressing afternoon in packing up, and had just finished when a letter arrived in his now familiar scrawl. I opened it listlessly, and then, as I read, my heart gave a bound. He was still busy, quite unable to return. Could I give him another week? And then there was a postscript. Had his mother and sister been again?

"A week?" I thought. He could have a month, a year, and I would never ask a fee. How I danced round the room! How I whistled and sang, and kicked the portmanteau under the bed, and dragged it out again, and tumbled my carefully-folded things upon the floor! And then I remembered I must tell Mrs Walsham the news, and I skipped downstairs and nearly into the arms of a man who was talking to her in the little passage. It was Inns' friend, the dark-bearded man.

"Look here!" he demanded. "I thought you told me Dr Inns would be home today?"

I should have resented the tone and the manner had I felt only a degree less exhilarated. As it was, I answered with equal stiffness.

"So I believed at the time I saw you."

"Have you got the least idea when he will be back?" He glanced as he spoke at the open letter I held. It was on the tip of my tongue to tell him, but I checked myself. Confound him! What right had he to speak to me like that?

"It is very uncertain," I replied, by no means uncandidly. "Will you leave any message this time?"

"No. I have to be in London immediately." And with a curt "Good-day," he disappeared.

In the agreeable task of answering Inns, I quite forgot this unpleasant incident. Indeed, it was only as an afterthought I made a casual reference to the man's visits, adding that Inns would no doubt be sorry to have missed his friend.

And now I began to torture myself with all my old doubts of again seeing Miss Innes (I learned the correct name later), and from that time, so fearful was I of being out of the way, that, except when on my few visits, I dared not stir a yard from the house.

The next day passed, and the next, and the next after that, before my devotion was rewarded. Yes, she came and how charming she looked! What I said, what I did, I cannot tell. All I know is that to her I spoke, at her I looked, and for a time I heard and saw no one else. I suppose I did not make a palpable fool of myself, for when I began to recover my balance Mrs Innes was speaking.

"We can only think he must have altered in some way. Something must have happened, some terrible disease or disfigurement; he has been abroad so much. Tell me, Dr Wilkinson, is it so? No? You have seen nothing of it? Oh, what a relief! But why this refusal to meet us? We cannot help seeing that he avoids us. He who used to be so devoted to us both, while we remember him only as the gentlest, noblest, most chivalrous of men!"

"Good Heavens!" I mentally exclaimed.

"And now," she continued, "I don't know what to think. There are only us three left, and he will not see us." She covered her face with her hands and sobbed. There was not a trace of her former stand-off manner now, and I felt genuinely sorry for her.

"Will you not help us, Dr Wilkinson?" Miss Innes had turned to me, her eyes brimming with tears. It made my blood boil to think that anyone, least of all a boor like Inns, should cause her such distress. Help her, indeed! I had a struggle not to fling myself at her feet and declare myself her devoted slave.

"Only tell me how, and I will do anything in the world!" I protested.

"Help us to meet him – that is all we ask," said she, smiling at my vehemence.

I thought a moment.

"I have agreed to stay here till the end of the week. If I telegraph on Friday that I must positively leave the next day that will bring him back, and you will be certain to find him on Saturday afternoon. If anything should occur to prevent this I could telegraph to you, Mrs Innes, if you will give me the address."

"I'm afraid I haven't got a card with me," said the elder lady after a hunt through her bag. "Will you write it down?"

I took out my pocketbook, when Miss Innes exclaimed, "I have a card."

The rest of the day I spent in striking futile matches in the endeavour to keep a pipe going. I suppose it looks foolish when set down in black and white, but it is a fact that I never took my eye from a white card, with "First and Third Wednesdays" in one corner, which I had stuck up on the mantel-piece where I could see it. Yes, I was very far gone indeed.

Mindful of my promise, after finishing the rounds on Friday I cycled on to Treacham to send Inns my ultimatum. Just as I got to the post-office I met the postman. He had a telegram for me, and was not at all sorry to be spared a four-mile tramp.

Opening it, I read: "Please stop on; detained till next week. Has friend called again?"

"No, no, Dr Inns," I thought. "I'm ready for you this time." And turning into the office I wired: "Quite impossible; must positively leave Saturday. Friend has returned to London. – Wilkinson."

The possession of a certain small square of cardboard, carefully treasured in my pocketbook, enabled me to pack up the next morning in a less dismal frame of mind than I had been in a week before.

When Inns arrived after mid-day, I greeted him with a cheerfulness which he appeared disinclined to reciprocate. He seemed more uncouth than ever, and growled something about breaking off negotiations for the sale through having to come back so soon.

In fact he was in a very bad temper, and I suspected he had been drinking. For when during lunch I referred to the cases of Ikin and Warkwell, and hinted ever so gently at their real states, he lost control of himself entirely. He flew into a violent passion and finally accused me of "trying to steal the practice from him!"

This was rather more than I could stand, so keeping a tight hand on myself I rose from the table and, telling him if he would be good enough to write me a cheque for the month's work I would leave at once, I went upstairs to finish packing.

As I left the room he roared something after me that sounded like "Not a penny!" I cared little what he said, for I knew his sober reason would tell him that I had the whip-hand of him, and he dare not allow me to sue him for the money.

I had very little more packing to do, and was about to carry the portmanteau down, when I heard a knock and then a voice which I recognised with a palpitating heart.

In my resentment with the drunken brute downstairs I had actually forgotten his mother and sister, and now, as ill-luck would have it, they had arrived at the very worst time they could have chosen. Inns was scarcely fit for the society of men, let alone ladies. I bitterly reproached myself for managing him with so little tact. But regrets being useless I stole downstairs at once, as I felt sure I should be wanted sooner or later. I could hear Inns growling in deeper and deeper bass, and just as I reached the door I heard the mother's voice.

"What have you done with him? You have murdered him!" she cried.

Something fell, and Miss Innes screamed for help. I rushed in, to find Inns clutching his mother by the throat. Seizing an overturned chair, the first thing handy, I dealt him a crack on the head that would have fractured any ordinary skull. He was not even stunned, however, but fell plump, like a sack of grain, into the corner, where he made no attempt to rise, but lay growling and cursing at large. When I turned round Mrs Innes and her daughter, both looking very pale, were clasping each other at the farther end of the room.

"Who is this man?" Mrs Innes demanded; and then as I stared at her, too bewildered to utter a word, "That is not my son!" she insisted.

At this moment there came a knock at the outer door, and a quick step approached along the passage. It was Inns' dark friend. For a second he stood surveying the scene, and then, with a cry of "Mother!" stretched out his arms as the two women sprang forward.

They clung to him with sobs and murmurs of "Reginald! My dear boy! Thank God, you've come back!"

Feebly wondering what was going to happen next, I turned to my late employer. The blow seemed to have sobered him, and except for a slight scalp wound, he was none the worse. I helped him to get up, for which he thanked me quite humbly, but he trembled and but for me would have fallen again when the stranger approached.

"And now, Jones," said the latter, "I should like to know what you mean by making use of my name."

"Well, sir, it's rather a long story."

"Thank you, I know the beginning of it. I heard you were sentenced to five years for defrauding your employers."

"Ah, it was a false charge, sir. Indeed it was! I'm as innocent as what you are. I managed to escape on my way to Portland, and as everyone thought you'd died after you disappeared from the ship, I thought there was no harm in taking your name. In order to keep up the disguise I took to doctoring, and I came down to this quiet place, as there wouldn't be much to do in the medical line.

"I'd put some money by before I got into trouble, and was living quiet and happy till these two ladies found me out. I've tried always to keep out of their sight, so they shouldn't give me away, but as I was afraid they'd see me after all one day, I've been trying to sell the practice and go abroad. If I hadn't been so flustered by their coming here and accusing me of murdering you I shouldn't have said what I did, and I humbly ask their pardon for it."

"So it seems you've been carrying on a bogus practice in my name. Well, if I can't clap you in prison for that I'll see if I can't send you back as an escaped convict."

"Oh, doctor, do let me go! I'll leave the country at once, and you shan't ever hear no more of me." And he grovelled abjectly at Innes' feet.

"Oh, let him go!" Mrs Innes pleaded.

"Very well, then; but as soon as I get back to London I go straight to Scotland Yard, and tell them all about you. Now get out! You've got a day's start."

As the ex-convict shuffled out of the room I made a movement to go also, but Innes stopped me.

"Don't go, Dr Wilkinson," said he. "I owe you an apology for what passed between us last week. I thought you were in league with that scoundrel, so I told you I was going back to London. But I only laid low and waited until I found he had returned. It's just four years since I was doctor on board the ship of which he was purser. I had a kind of sunstroke at Buenos Ayres, and was picked up in the street and taken to a hospital. Meanwhile the ship sailed without me, for I had lost my memory and couldn't say anything about myself – I only remembered my name by the mark on my linen!

"Well, I had to do something, so I went up country and got work on a cattle-ranch and eventually I got all right again. By the time I had saved some money and began to think of coming home, nearly three years had gone. I wrote twice to you, mother, but never got an answer. I found when I reached home you had moved twice, and I couldn't trace you. I was very worried, of course, at that. And what was worse was the seeing my name in the *Medical Directory* as in practice at this place. I really thought my brain was affected when I read that! I never suspected the truth until I took a run down here and made some inquiries. He might at least have pronounced my name properly! Hulloa! What's that?"

There was a sound of galloping, and we all ran to the door as Jones, in frenzied haste, took flight in the pony-cart.

"A good riddance!" was Innes' benediction.

"By Jove, though, he never gave me my cheque!" I exclaimed.

"Oh, I'll see to that. I must take over the debts with the rest of the practice," laughed Innes.

# How I Cured a
# Hopeless Paralytic

I used to think some years ago that I was tolerably proof against most infections, including that of influenza. But I suppose I had got into a "receptive condition," for I had not long been back in my rooms after my last engagement before I began to feel a most unmistakable seediness. My old friend Nosbury, whom I consulted, in a kindly-meant effort to relieve my depression was inclined to put the symptoms down to over-smoking. But when he took my temperature and caught a glimpse of that blankety tongue he sent me to bed straight-away, and there I stayed for a fortnight on end.

There was nothing special about the attack. It ran its usual course, but as a result of a month's enforced idleness, to say nothing of the incidental expenses, I found I had made a larger hole in my small capital than I was able to contemplate unmoved. Just in the nick of time, and when I was thinking of spending a few pounds more on a recruiting trip to Brighton, Adamson – that prince of agents! – offered me the charge of a practice in the New Forest. He described it as "small and easy," and I was only too glad to take it, small and easy as the fee might also prove.

When I got down to Rougholt I found that Adamson's expression was not a mere epigram. Dr Wild was a man of some means, and appeared to practise more for the sake of an occupation than anything else. He was an active member of the Alpine Club and I barely saw him before he was off for his holiday to Switzerland.

Personally, I am of that not inconsiderable class in whom altitudes create a horrid sensation of fear and discomfort, and I was unable to understand why a man who appeared to enjoy so many of the good things of life should risk his neck among the gulfs and precipices whose pictures covered the walls of nearly every room in the house. Mrs Wild, who was an equally expert Alpinist, accompanied her husband, and as they had no family I was left practically master of the house – a state of things in which, judging by past experience, the advantages and disadvantages were about equally balanced.

The work, when I had once got used to it, proved to be so light that I began to look on it as an agreeable opportunity for getting up my strength for more serious work, although as matters turned out it was by no means a sinecure. But the chief attraction of the place, I may as well say at once, was that Rougholt lay an easy cycle-ride from Southampton, where I knew Mrs Innes had taken a house.

I had seen very little of the Innes family in town, my wretched illness being responsible for much. But I had seen enough to convince me that Louise was the one woman on earth for me, and it was only the uncertainty of my position which kept me from telling her in so many words what feminine intuition must have enabled her to see long ago.

As I said, the work to begin with was very light, the patients being mostly old chronic cases who only needed visiting at regular intervals. There was one, however, who interested me more from the surrounding circumstances than from any inherent attraction of his disease. Artlett had been a labourer in the service of a neighbouring landowner, and about eighteen months before I made his acquaintance he had received some kind of injury to his back while working a steam-plough. There seemed little amiss with him at first, so I gathered, but he had gradually developed a paralysis of the lower limbs, and now was hopelessly bed-ridden.

His master was locally known as a "hard man," and Artlett, without waiting to see what might be done for his relief, seemed to have jumped to the conclusion that there was nothing before him but the workhouse. Partly influenced by friends, but chiefly by the unscrupulous advice of a shady Southampton solicitor, he took proceedings under the Employers' Liability Act. Although the case was not at all a clear one, and in spite of adverse medical evidence, he had ended in scoring off his old master to the tune of a pound a week. Of his employer of course I knew nothing, but I was disgusted by the way in which Artlet plumed himself on his astuteness as with true rustic cunning he told the story.

The judge, he was a prime one, he was; *he* wouldn't let the doctor say there was nothing the matter with him; *he* stood up for the working man, he did – bless him! Such, or something like it, with additions, was the gist of his paean, and after a few visits I knew it well enough to repeat backwards.

I am sure that had his late master heard but a little of what was dinned into my ears there would have been a drying-up of the stream of comforts with which, for all his "hardness," he kept Artlett supplied. Not a day passed without something arriving from the Hall. Jellies, soups, custards, now a chicken, then a small joint; Artlett's menus must have been the most luxurious in any cottage in the country.

So far as cooking was concerned, Artlett's daughter had a sinecure which she fully appreciated, as I hardly ever found her at home. Her father was always whining about her "gaddings out," and grimly prophesying as to the fate in store for a girl with too many strings to her bow. As a widower, no doubt he felt this neglect of his sole companion, and for this reason I visited him more often than perhaps was necessary. I soon wished, however, that he had another topic of conversation than his County Court suit, even though it had been the great event of his life.

With absolutely none of the minor troubles which assail the paralysed, Artlett was, on the whole, a very healthy man, were it not for a chronic dyspepsia, which I put down to the endless procession of dainties from the Hall. I was not sorry to find in him something that I could treat, for his paralysis was quite hopeless. He was fond of reciting in self-pity that "physicians were in vain," and some other things that might in consequence be anticipated. But it was not long before his symptoms began to puzzle me.

I had been attending him about a week when he drew my attention one day to what he called a "new paralis," and truly he had some loss of power in the right wrist which he was unable to straighten. He seemed much upset about it, and inclined to ascribe it to a spreading of the original injury, but that I knew to be very unlikely. Besides, this new trouble made me suspect something entirely different. I took the opportunity of thoroughly overhauling him, and was not very much surprised to detect a blue line round the gums.

To save time, I may as well say that the symptoms pointed to chronic lead-poisoning. Most people nowadays know that this is a very common disease, and a few years ago, when leaden vessels were extensively used, it was even commoner than at present. The principal signs are chronic indigestion with a bluish line round the gums and a paralysis of the extending muscles of the forearm leading to the "drop-wrist," which is so characteristic of the disease. All these I found present in Artlett.

As a principal cause of the poisoning is water conveyed in lead-pipes, I questioned him as to the water supply, but found that it all came from a deep well, and when I had a look round the premises later on I saw no reason to suspect either the well or the wooden bucket which was used in it. Besides, Artlett was not a water-drinker, and, as I have already hinted, little or no water was required for cooking. So I tried to cheer him up as much as possible, and when I got home prescribed the usual remedies for the case.

When I saw him the next day Artlett was very depressed. He appeared to resent the fact of his being no better, although of course it was absurd to expect any immediate change. However, as he had given me a taste of his quality, I knew it behoved me to be very circumspect, and, without telling him the real nature of the case, I inquired very carefully into his habits and way of living.

He stared somewhat when I expressed a wish to take samples of his food away with me, although with rustic caution he said little. I told him a yarn I had concocted about the treatment of chronic dyspepsia and endeavoured to explain the process of digestion. He evidently understood little of what I said, although he appeared greatly impressed. In the end I requisitioned all the empty medicine bottles I could find, and stowed quite a number of samples of food and drink, not forgetting some water from the well, under the seat of the dog-cart. I was not cycling that day, having a longer round than usual.

The next morning I was sent for in quite another direction, and in the afternoon I had to do what I should have otherwise done in the morning, so that I was unable to work around to Artlett until the evening.

A little way from the house his daughter met me – she was at home for a wonder – and told me a curious piece of news. Her father appeared to have been much upset by my proceedings of the day before. She had found him behaving like a madman more than anything else – in fact had been quite afraid to remain in the house with him. He had been abusing doctors and everyone, so she didn't think it would be safe for me to see him. He had refused all food, and had eaten nothing since yesterday but some bread and milk she had made for him herself. When she offered him some fish from the Hall, the same as he used to be so fond of, he had thrown it in the fire, using "dreadful language."

I was very interested in this new development. It was not long before that I had read of insanity arising as a result of lead-poisoning. I endeavoured to calm the daughter's fears, and promised to be as soothing as I knew with the patient. When I got into the room I could see little outward change, and Artlett greeted me very much as usual. I talked on indifferent matters as long as possible, but it was inevitable that the subject which was occupying both our minds should crop up sooner or later.

"Look here, doctor," he suddenly burst out. "I wants to speak to yer like a man. Yes, yes! I know what ye're going to say, but I want yer to answer me like a man. There's something going on I don't understand."

"I don't suppose you do, Artlett, but – "

"It's not my trade, you're going to say, doctor. But it's your'n, and I pays yer to tell me!"

Now this was not only insulting but untrue, for his late employer was paying for the attendance. But I let it pass and merely said, "Well, what is it you want to know? Don't excite yourself so. We shall never get any further tonight if you don't keep calm."

"About this 'ere paralis, then?"

"Well, I think you've been taking something that hasn't agreed with you."

"That's it! It's the bile on the brain! I feels it playin' on me more and more every day."

"What are you talking about, Artlett?"

"They're poisonin' of me! Rot 'em!"

"Poisoning you?"

"Ah, I knows all about it! Yer may shake yer 'ead, but yer knows it too."

"I tell you, Artlett, I don't know what you mean."

"What did yer put in all them bottles, then, what yer took 'ome with yer?"

"Why, you saw what I put in them!"

"Ah, I knows! And what did yer find in 'em?"

"Nothing!" This was rather more than the truth, for of course I had had no time to analyse the samples.

"I knows better. 'E's poisonin' of me!"

"Who is? Once more, say what you mean and have done with it."

"Why, Mr Kirtley, to be sure."

"You must be mad! Isn't he doing all he can to keep you alive, and paying you into the bargain?"

"That's it!" he roared. "'E wants ter stop a-payin' me as he's got to by law – County Court law. 'E wants to get rid of me!"

I was so astounded that, unfortunately, the old fox saw my embarrassment.

"Well, yer knows it, doctor!" he cried. "What did yer take all them things away for? All them victuals 'e sends me? Sech a kind gen'l'man as 'e is! Look at my pore 'and! 'E stole my legs, an' now 'e's stealin' my arms! 'E'll soon 'ave my life! Rot 'im!"

I noticed, with a good deal of interest, that his mental disturbance seemed to overcome his physical helplessness, for his legs twitched violently under the bed-clothes as he swayed to and fro in his excitement. Presently he began to whimper, and I seized the opportunity to argue with him.

"Look here, Artlett," I said. "I'm quite sure that you're talking utter nonsense. Mr Kirtley is far too rich a man to notice the loss of what he pays you, even if he were wicked enough to try and kill you. And as to that, it's simply absurd! But if you think so – "

"It's gospel-truth, and yer knows it!"

"Well, well, let me finish. The thing for you to do is very simple. If you think you're being poisoned, don't take any food but what your daughter buys and cooks for you. Keep on with the medicine, and I'll send a draught to quiet you down."

"I won't take no more physic! You're as bad as what 'e is!"

I could see it was a waste of time to argue with him. With all the prejudice and suspicion of his class he seemed to consider his master quite capable of what he might probably have done himself had their positions been reversed.

As I rode homeward I hardly knew what to make of it all. It would have been strange indeed if Artlett had stumbled on the true cause of his lead-poisoning. His ideas of foul play were, of course, ridiculous, but it was quite possible that he was being poisoned in all innocence – literally killed by kindness! It was clear that I must analyse these samples without loss of time.

Several things delayed me when I got back, but as soon as I had half-an-hour to spare I set to work and made the most exhaustive analysis possible with the limited appliances at hand. Fortunately, lead is a substance very easily detected by chemical tests, and although it was a tedious process away from an analyst's laboratory, by the time I had finished I felt satisfied I had left no stone unturned in my search. In a word, I was unable to find the slightest trace of lead in any of the food samples; all were of equal innocence, while the water, as I had expected, was above suspicion.

I felt more puzzled than ever – indeed, the word feebly describes my state of mind as I surveyed the squad of bottles whose contents I had banned with such haste. As to the nature of Artlett's new complaint, there could be no question. I doubt if a junior student would have hesitated before giving a correct diagnosis; yet of the origin of the disease I was absolutely ignorant.

When I visited Artlett the next day I found him more amenable to reason. For one thing, although his wrist was unaltered, his other symptoms were relieved – a fact which he attributed to his home-made diet, although I solemnly assured him he need have no dread of the delicacies from the Hall. As his daughter took occasion to inform me that she had persuaded him to continue my treatment, I got him to admit that I might possibly have done him some good, and with that I left him.

I now come to the curious experience which resulted in such an addition to the work at Rougholt. Two or three days afterwards I was called out to Stonewood, a village about four miles off. The patient was of the average type of agricultural labourer, deliberate of speech and slow of comprehension, his symptoms striking me as rather anomalous until I came to examine the mouth, and there found the familiar blue line, plain and unmistakable, around the gums. I could learn little that was of any use in deciding the origin of his trouble, so I took a sample of the drinking water. It was from a cistern in this case.

On getting home I tested for lead without results, and began to wonder whether the chemicals or my ignorance were responsible for my failure.

When I visited the patient the next day his wife told me that I was wanted at another house in the village. This was the little general-store, and the proprietor gave me such an account of himself as led me to suspect his mouth also. There was the blue line in all its beauty, but, as before, I learned nothing to account for it, and finally returned with another sample of water.

By this time I was growing used to negative results of my analyses, and as the matter was becoming serious I determined to take the samples with me to Southampton and see what a professional analyst could make of it. There were other reasons moving me to this expedition; but, honestly, Wild's chemicals were not above suspicion of antiquity and consequent inertia.

I had arranged the next morning's work with the idea of getting over to Southampton early. Artlett, though still convinced of the reality of the plot against him, alluded to it in a less actively volcanic style. Both in Artlett's case and that of the Stonewood men, there was really little to be done until I had managed to discover the true source of the lead-poisoning. If anything cropped up to detain me I had thought of putting off the two latter visits till the afternoon, although Artlett I intended to see early in any case.

I still have a vivid recollection of the intense disgust I felt when on coming down to breakfast I found waiting for me not one message only, but three. All were from Stonewood, too, and all fresh cases!

My trip to Southampton bade fair to be a mere ride to the analyst's and back again, if, indeed, I ever got there at all. However, there was no help for it. The life of a medical man is one long string of self-denials! I recalled somewhat bitterly an old theory of mine: how much more essential to a doctor than a priest was a life of celibacy, the softer and more intimate relations of life being so constantly supplanted by the calls of professional duty, if not of humanity.

I packed my carrier with the samples I had accumulated in the last few days, and having assured Artlett, quite uselessly, that the murder plot had extended to Stonewood, I rode on there and lost no time in visiting the first new patient. He was a blacksmith, and I was more than startled by the strong family likeness of his symptoms to those of the others in the village. He had been a fighting-man, I learned, and had lost all his teeth in early life, so there was little hospitality for the blue line on his gums. All the same, I felt certain that it ought to have been there.

Wondering what I should discover next, I went on to an agricultural labourer's cottage. He was a trifle more intelligent than the one I saw at first, who, by the way, lived next door to him. When I came to examine him I was astounded to find all the familiar symptoms as well marked as in any of the others! I was speechless – a fact which, I afterwards learnt, had greatly impressed the patient, with whom my reputation for profound wisdom was established for all time.

Somehow or other, I managed to find my way through the village to the "Goose and Gridiron," whence the third message came. Here I saw the youth who was barman and general factotum of the little ale-house, kept by a widow. By this time I might have been excused had I regarded every ailment of the Stonewood men as proof of lead-poisoning. When the ostler commenced to talk of his indigestion, his inability to pull the beer-engine or to move a barrel, and finally exhibited the nerveless droop of his wrist, I had no need of the blue line upon his gums to convince me that he, too, had succumbed to the prevailing malady.

I had no faculty of amazement left now. Never had I seen anything like it! The disease had assumed the proportions of an epidemic. I felt it was getting on my nerves, and that I must have a positive analysis of my specimens at once. And so, having taken a sample of the water from the "Goose and Gridiron," I looked in on the two old patients, and then rode on to Southampton with my carrier full of rattling bottles.

I lunched at the "Star" in High Street, and leaving the machine there, took my samples to the firm of wholesale druggists whom Wild dealt with. It was but a very simple analysis that was wanted, and I felt both pleased and vexed when they discovered no more than myself – pleased that my chemical knowledge had not grown rusty, and very much annoyed to be unrelieved of my incubus. This matter disposed of, I dawdled round till the conventional visiting hour.

From my first visit to the Innes' in London they had let me see very plainly that I was not their most unwelcome visitor. Remembering all the circumstances of our acquaintance, it would have been strange had I been otherwise. But I was for ever doubting whether this cordiality, on the part of Miss Innes, at least, was anything more than gratitude for past services, and whether I would imperil my footing in the house by any attempt to render it a more intimate one. And now, today, at Southampton, I was filled with new alarms.

On a former visit I had met a certain Major Johnstone of the Army Medical Department – an excellent fellow, by the way – and finding him there again I must needs imagine all sorts of half-hidden familiarities between him and Louise, and so began to cordially detest him. But I was in love, and therefore to some extent irresponsible. I thought of salving my peace of mind by seeing my military friend out. But it was no good; and when Mrs Innes spoke of asking him to witness some share transfers, I thought I had discovered a possible hint, and so rose to go. But the elder lady would by no means hear of this, and in a little time Louise and I were alone.

Why is it that when a man is most anxious to shine he is pretty sure to make an ass of himself? Here was the opportunity I had long looked for. I had rehearsed the scene over and over again in my mind. It all ran so smoothly when I was alone, but now – !

My throat seemed parched, and my tongue dry. I wished I had never taken that sherry at lunch. My collar felt tight, too – strange I had never noticed it before! And worst of all, my nose began to itch! This was horrible, for to scratch it would spoil the situation for ever!

How I wished Miss Innes would go away, if only for a moment, so that I might get into fighting trim, so to speak. I suppose she noticed my embarrassment, for, tactful as ever, she made conversation. Dr Johnstone was such a charming man (*confound him!*); an old friend of her father's and his executor (*good – that explained his frequent presence*); he had married a cousin of theirs (*blessings on him!*).

I was so delighted to hear this that I found my tongue again with the doltish remark, "Ah, I wondered why he was here so much!"

Her eyes beneath her perfectly arched brows met mine with a look of calm inquiry; those wonderful eyes, fathomless abysses, as they had seemed the first time I saw her! What an impertinent fool I must seem! And, trying, to better matters, I floundered dismally.

"No, I don't mean that! I thought – I mean I was afraid he was – Miss Innes, I want to tell you that you are always in my thoughts."

My tongue felt like a thong of leather. Suddenly I remembered a sentence I had rehearsed often enough, and in a voice which I intended to sound thrilling, but which was only sepulchral, went on:

"Louise, may I hope you are not indifferent to me?" How tame and flat it sounded after I had got it off! And the dear girl never laughed.

"You have known me such a short time," she said quite frankly.

"Why, it seems ages!" I protested, and encouraged by the tone I seemed able to detect in her voice, I hunted for another speech from my repertory. How did it run? Oh, yes! If the devotion of a lifetime −. But just as I opened my mouth she raised her hand warningly, as her mother entered, and saved me from making an absolute fool of myself.

Now that I knew Johnstone to be harmless I felt so cordially disposed towards him that I could have embraced him on the spot. I wondered afterwards whether the reaction from my previous excitement had made me unduly demonstrative. We were certainly a very merry party, and Johnstone came out as a most entertaining *raconteur*.

But what born actresses are women! Not the slightest sign of emotion, except perhaps in a little deepening of colour, did Louise show as a result of what had just passed. The barely-returned pressure as I took her hand in parting was my sole assurance that there existed an understanding between us.

I was not so elated with my good fortune as to be oblivious of everything else. I was but a little distance on my way back before I was deep in consideration of the Stonewood epidemic. Approaching the village, the sign of the "Goose and Gridiron" was conspicuous, and the sight suggested an entirely new idea. As I had tested the water for lead unsuccessfully, why not examine another kind of beverage? I would extend my researches to the beer. Its consumption was certainly more extensive and popular than that of the water. Dismounting, I walked into the bar, where my latest patient sat spelling out a glove-contest in a weekly paper while a fat, pursy old woman dozed in the parlour behind.

"Good evening, sir. Want any refreshment?"

"Not just now, thanks, but I should like to have a bottle of your ale to take home with me."

"Which'll you have?"

"Oh, I don't know. Which do you take yourself?"

"I mostly take the thruppenny."

"And what do Puddy and Williams fancy?" naming the blacksmith and the general shop man.

"Their fancy's the same – real old Burton," slapping the handle of the beer-engine. And then, as he filled a bottle for me, "How be Mr Artlett now?"

"Pretty well. Do you know him?"

"Oh, yes. I knows 'im!" adding, in a stage whisper, as he jerked his thumb towards the parlour, "'E's a-sparkin' the missus! Banns are a-goin' up soon."

"But I mean Artlett – the paralysed man, you know."

"Oh, yes; that's 'im. We all knows about that there," he added with a subtle grin.

As I rode off with the bottle of beer I tried to picture the dalliance of the bed-ridden Artlett and the fat ale-wife, who presumably was an occasional visitor to the cottage. True, their attachment could hardly rest upon what De Quincey has styled "a tenure so perishable as mere personal beauty," but Artlett enjoyed what was practically a life pension, "by County Court law," as he would have put it, enabling him to rank as a man of substance. And the beer-shop would endow the widow with attractions which the grossest flattery must deny to her person.

Just outside the village I punctured badly, and when I got down to investigate I found I had run over one of those diabolical iron boot-tips, which had entered the tyre with all its three teeth. More, they had gone through the opposite side of the tube, for when, after a most elaborate repair, I replaced the tyre and inflated, for all my pumping I was no further forward. So off the tyre had to come again, while I did another and even larger patching. It could not have been more than six when I punctured, but by the time I had finished the sun had long set, and dusk was coming on fast.

I lit my lamp and pedalled hard. There was no time to lose. I was not to know what might be happening in my absence, and I had been away since noon.

"Where yer comin' to?" someone shouted, suddenly.

*Crash!*

I went flying from the cycle. When I scrambled out of the ditch – there had been no rain of late and it was quite dry, thank goodness – the lamp was still burning on the machine as it lay far along the road. I was just able to make out the figure of the man I had run into, sitting upon a stone-heap. I was none the worse for the spill, though a bit shaken.

"I'll soon see you – I'm a doctor," I called to him, and ran to the machine. I was relieved to find both it and the bottle of beer were safe and sound, so dragging it to the side of the road, I unshipped the lamp and went back to the man.

He had disappeared! At first I thought I had mistaken the spot and hunted about for another. But no, here was the patch of roadway I had swept as I skimmed into the ditch, and opposite was the heap of stones where I could swear I had seen the man holding his head and growling at me.

At my feet something shone brightly as I flashed the lamp about. I picked it up; it was a brass tobacco-box, a broken clay pipe beside it. But for this evidence of the collision, I might have almost doubted its occurrence, in such ghostly fashion had the obstructionist vanished. Pocketing the box, I remounted a little stiffly, and rode on to Rougholt.

After the moving events of the day I slept soundly, but my earliest waking thought was of the beer, and scarcely waiting to swallow breakfast, I set to work examining it. Although I was inclined to distrust the chemicals, they played me no tricks. A few minutes' testing showed a marked reaction of lead in the sample, and then – I had solved the mystery!

It lay in the cellars of the "Goose and Gridiron," or rather, in the leaden pipes through which the beer was drawn from the barrels. But the next minute my enthusiasm evaporated, as I thought of Artlett. How was I to account for his share in the epidemic? He lay a good three miles from the alehouse, and the beer he drank, until the last few days at least, was supplied by the Hall.

Suddenly I bethought me of the tapster's remark, of the "sparking," and of the approaching publication of the banns. Here was a possible connection with the "Goose and Gridiron," which I must do my best to investigate.

"Why, what on earth is the matter with you?" I exclaimed when, a couple of hours later, I visited Artlett. His left eye was completely closed by an acute swelling of the lids, a strip of postage-stamp paper concealed what appeared to be a cut across the brow, while his head was swathed in vinegar-soaked rags.

"Ah! Mr Kirtley was like to get his heart's desire last night."

"Whatever do you mean, Artlett? And, once and for all, I must ask you to drop that absurd idea about Mr Kirtley – at any rate, when you are speaking to me."

"I was near bein' burnt alive! I was lyin' readin' the Bible last night when the candle tipped over on the bed, and a-tryin' to pick it up again I pitched clean out on my 'ead."

"You must have had a job to get back again."

"Ah, you're right! It was a job, I can tell you."

"You won't look in very good trim for the wedding," I suggested wickedly.

He leered at me suspiciously out of the corner of his eye, then after a pause said: "Oh, my darter ain't goin' to be married yet awhile."

"No, no, Artlett," I persisted. "Don't be bashful. I'm talking of *your* wedding. How are you going to reach the church?"

"Suppose I'll get there some'ow."

I could see the old fox hardly relished the turn the conversation had taken, but I continued ruthlessly.

"I should think that the landlady will be able to get some sort of conveyance from Stonewood for you."

"I've looked everywhere for it, father, and I can't stop any longer – Oh, I beg your pardon, sir!" Artlett's daughter, a flutter of ribbons and cheap finery, burst in upon us at this point, to his evident relief.

"How do you think he is, sir? He's lost his tobacco-box, but I don't think he ought to smoke – ought he?"

I remembered the prize I had secured in my encounter the previous night with the vanishing rustic.

"Here's one you can have," said I, pulling it from my pocket.

"Why, there it is!" exclaimed the daughter. "Wherever did you find it, sir?"

"No, it ain't! I tell yer it ain't!" protested Artlett vehemently, as I offered him the box which he refused to even look at.

"Yes, it is, father. Don't be so stupid! Why see!" She took it from me. "Here's EA for 'Ebenezer Artlett,' what you scratched on yourself. Did you find it outside, sir?"

"I picked it up last night in the road. It must have been dropped by a man I ran into on my bicycle. Why, Artlett, could that have been you? How on earth –!"

I felt bewildered as a rush of new ideas and suspicions crowded upon me, and stopped short. As for Artlett, he was clearly in a state of great excitement. His face had turned pallid. Even the ruby of his inflamed eyelid had blanched, while he trembled so violently that the bedstead rattled.

"Have you nothing handy to give him – something warm?" I glanced to the hob, where a little pipkin simmered.

"Here, father – come now! Take this." She had dipped into the vessel and was offering him a basin of steaming gruel.

Turning to me, she said, "It's all he lives on now, sir, since he won't take the things from the Hall."

Artlett was tremulously waving her away, and as the girl turned to me I suppose in his agitation must have struck her arm. Anyhow, the basin slipped from her hands, and in a moment the scalding fluid deluged the bed-clothes, thin and flimsy as they were, that covered his shanks.

Whatever the girl may have expected, I was certainly not prepared for the transformation which the accident effected. One moment a bed-ridden cripple lay before us; the next, with a yell of agony, he had bounded from the bed. Before either of us could move a finger to detain him, he rushed madly to the door at the moment a well-dressed man appeared on the threshold. Turning short off with a rustic oath, the recent paralytic vaulted over the bed again with the agility of an acrobat. Darting through the back door, he disappeared in the yard behind with his daughter now in pursuit.

For a second or two the new arrival and I stared at one another in amazement. Then as the full absurdity of the situation dawned upon us, we both burst into a roar of laughter, which at once thawed all formality.

The stranger was the first to recover his gravity.

"I think you are Dr Wild's *locum tenens?*" he asked as he wiped the tears from his eyes. "I must congratulate you on the brilliant success of your treatment in unmasking an impostor."

"You know him, then?" I gasped, as soon as I had breath to speak.

"Very well indeed! My name is Kirtley."

# How I Helped to Lay a Ghost

"Well, Jarvis, anything the matter at the stable?" I asked, as the coachman entered rather breathlessly.

"No, sir; it's at the bank."

"The bank!" I echoed. "Why, they closed long ago, didn't they?"

"Yes, sir; that is, not altogether, sir. As I passed there, coming back from tea, I saw Mr Major, the constable, who asked me to come and fetch you at once, as someone was hurt."

I was at Ashtreecroft, in West Berks, a little north of the Hants border, and I have seen few prettier spots even in that region of picturesque villages. I had heard of the practice from the agent as one that was growing rather beyond the single-handed powers of Sayfield, its owner. As I had always had the idea of a partnership as the most satisfactory way of purchasing a practice, I agreed to take charge for a month to learn the best and worst it had to offer.

The fact is, I was beginning to chafe at my perpetual packing up and moving on – one month here, another there, for all the world like a strolling player. Now that Miss Innes had become such an important factor in my life, I pined more than ever for a settled habitation.

Nothing calling for particular notice occurred during the greater part of the first month. Indeed, had it not been for the special interest I took in what I began to regard as my own practice, the work might have seemed monotonous. It was not until the third week of my stay that the event I am about to relate took place.

It was now the third Wednesday, a date I remember for this reason: the business at Ashtreecroft being small, the bank, which was but a branch of a larger establishment at Reading, only opened on the Wednesday market-day. The office was on the ground floor of a little house in what would, had the village been of more importance, have attained the rank of the High Street. But as the only thoroughfare of the place it had no name, and the word "Bank" on the window was all that guided customers to what seemed in other respects a private residence.

"Mr Major is waiting for you in the yard, doctor," said the policeman standing at the door, which he carefully shut behind me. He then led the way to a cobble-paved yard at the back, which opened into an alley running parallel with the High Street, as I had better call it. Here I found the senior constable endeavouring by threats and entreaties to clear the premises of a little group of villagers, unwilling to be deprived of a spectacle about as interesting in their dull lives as a travelling circus.

The centre of attraction was the prostrate body of a young man, lying, apparently lifeless, by the back door of the bank. Posting my guide as sentinel over the alley-way, his superior greeted me silently, and helped me to turn over the man, who, I was relieved to find, was still breathing. He was neatly dressed in a dark flannel lounge-suit and, well groomed and spruce, showed no apparent signs of any violence.

"Attempted murder, I should say, sir," observed the constable, drawing a revolver from his pocket.

"Did you find that here?" I asked.

"Yes, lying a little way nearer the door." He handed me the weapon, of which only one chamber had apparently been loaded and discharged, the others being quite clear and empty.

As I turned the body over in search of any wound which might account for his condition, I asked: "Do you know him?"

"Oh, yes, sir! It's young Mr Meadowcroft, from the Reading bank. He drives over every week on market-day, and goes back in the afternoon."

Although with Major's help I examined the body thoroughly, carefully scanning the clothing for blood-marks, there was no evidence of haemorrhage, as would be inevitable from a revolver wound, nor could I see any other trace of violence. There was certainly an abrasion on the left side of his forehead. Major, when I questioned him, remembered that when first seen that was the side upon which the body lay. But the fact went for little in the presence of the discharged revolver.

"How came you to discover him?" I asked.

"Well, sir, Edwards, my assistant, walking by about five-thirty, noticed that the bank window hadn't been shut, although the door was closed – they always shut it all up at three o'clock. So he knocked to remind old Wells, the porter. But as he didn't get any answer, he strolled along and came round the back way, expecting to find Wells somewhere about, as he sleeps on the premises. When he got to the back-yard gate it was standing open, and when he looked in, there was the young gentleman lying just as you found him."

"And no one about?"

"Not a soul! The back door of the house was open, and Edwards peeped in and called for Wells. But as he didn't come, he went out and sent a boy round to fetch me. As soon as I saw what had happened I sent Edwards off for you at once. But he met Dr Sayfield's man just outside, and when he came back I left him in charge of the body while I went into the bank and had a look round. There was no sign of Wells, though I hunted all over the house for him, and shouted loud enough to be heard in the street."

"But what about the revolver shot? Did no one hear it?"

"Ah! That's just it. You see, no one would be about but Wells. Mrs Bell there," jerking his head towards the crowd which now seemed to embrace most of the village, "she said just now she heard something, but thought it was the door banging, and just after that she heard the trap drive away as usual."

"Who would be driving?"

"Well, Mr Meadowcroft drives over from Reading in the trap in the morning, and they puts it under that shed there in the corner. They turns the horse into the stable-place, and Wells puts it to at three o'clock or so ready for Mr Meadowcroft to go back. I'm thinking he was just going to start when this happened, for Mrs Bell says it was some time between three and four she heard the wheels go. When I looked over the bank just now, it was all tidy, and no books or anything about, just as if Mr Meadowcroft had cleared everything up."

"But where is his hat?"

"Just so, sir. And I know he always comes over with some books and a bag – I suppose with some money in it. I've seen him with them often, but they're nowhere about inside."

"Whose is the revolver?"

"That I can't say."

"Well, he doesn't seem to be coming round," I remarked. "We had better take him inside and put him to bed."

"But who's going to look after him?" Major objected.

"Why, is there no one living here?"

"Only Wells, and he's a bachelor."

"Awkward!" I remarked. "Well, anyhow, we can't leave him here. There's no cottage-hospital or anything like that in the place, is there?"

"No, sir; no nearer than Reading."

"I suppose you have an ambulance, anyhow?"

"Yes, at the police station."

"Well, if you can bring him along to Dr Sayfield's, I'll see if we can't put him up there – at any rate, until he is fit to send to his own place."

I was myself occupying the spare room, but I arranged with the housekeeper to give it up to Meadowcroft while I turned into Sayfield's room. As the rooms adjoined, the arrangement was a convenient one, enabling me to keep a constant eye on the patient.

As it happened, we had scarcely got him undressed and put to bed before consciousness returned, and I was able to overhaul him thoroughly. I had already pretty well decided in my own mind that whatever else the revolver bullet had done, it had certainly inflicted no damage on Meadowcroft. After a further examination of him, I was not surprised that he complained of little beyond a severe headache and tenderness all along his left side. The bruise on his forehead was now quite apparent, and I suspected him to have been stunned by some blunt instrument. Anyhow, his memory was quite a blank at present, and as he seemed drowsy and inclined to sleep, I prescribed perfect rest and quietude. I reassured him as to his position, and left nature to do her own work. When I took an occasional peep at him during the evening he was sleeping soundly.

I was having a quiet smoke in the garden after dinner, when Major was announced. He had not come, it appeared, in quest of information so much as to impart it, for when I told him how well Meadowcroft was doing, he shook his head.

"Ah! A bad business, I'm afraid, sir."

"Not anyone shot, I hope?"

"No, but I've had a wire from the manager of the Reading bank to ask what's become of Mr Meadowcroft. I was just going to wire him myself when the message came. He says the horse was found wandering with the empty trap close to home, so I've only come to ask if I shall say that Mr Meadowcroft is doing well, and he can see him tomorrow."

"Yes, I think you may safely say he is getting on all right, but I don't think he will be fit to see anybody tomorrow."

As I expected, so it turned out. The next morning Meadowcroft still showed a little mental confusion, and I decided to keep him for at least another day in the seclusion of his darkened room. So when Major sent his subordinate to ask if he might bring the Reading manager to see him, I was inflexible in refusing.

Edwards told me that the horse was found grazing by the roadside near Reading. The books were safe inside, but a black leather bag with the cash was missing. He also added the curious fact that the clerk's hat was discovered lying at the bottom of the trap. He got this, he said, from the manager, who had brought over a new porter – a married man this time, whom he had installed in place of the missing Wells.

The day after, Meadowcroft was so much better that I allowed him to get up, but still thought it best to keep him to his room. He would have been quite reminiscent if I had suffered him, but I would not listen, telling him to reserve his story for the manager. The latter, when he arrived in the evening, proved not to be a very starched official, and I was pleased to see he greeted Meadowcroft in most friendly style.

"This is a change of scene, Mr Herbert," said the poor fellow.

"Never mind; it might have been worse. I'm glad to find you as well as this. Do you mind my asking him what he remembers, doctor? Thank you. Well now, Meadowcroft, was there anything particular in the afternoon?"

"No, nothing particular. Just the ordinary business."

"When did you close?"

"At three as usual. I had cleared everything up at three-thirty, and told Wells to get the horse put to. I remember collecting the books and taking them out to the cart, and then I got in with the bag."

"There was about five hundred pounds in it, wasn't there? At least, that is the amount I make it from the books."

"Yes. I remember now it was about three hundred pounds in notes and two hundred in cheques and bills paid in by the customers. Except for the cheques and so on, I was going back with about as much as I brought."

"Well, what then?"

There was a long silence. I could see the clerk racking his brain for a glimmer of recollection, and was just going to put a stop to the catechism when he flung his arms wide with a hopeless gesture.

"It's no use!" he exclaimed. "I really don't know what happened next! Everything seems a blank after that. Tell me, how long ago was it?"

"Never mind that for the present," I said. "Can you tell us what Wells did?"

"I can't say at all."

"Do you remember where he went to?" asked the manager.

"No; but why don't you ask him that?"

At this point I thought it time to interfere. Meadowcroft was becoming unduly excited. Obviously he had told all he knew, which, after all, was rather less than the manager seemed to know already. In the weak state of his brain it was not only cruel but dangerous to worry him with further questions. And to let him guess the real state of affairs might undo all the good of the rest and treatment I had been giving him.

"It certainly is a most mysterious affair," said the manager presently, as we sat together in the consulting room. "I would have trusted Wells to any extent. He was an old army man of exemplary character, and the last man on earth I should have suspected of robbing the bank, still less of adding murder to his crime. Yet still everything seems to point to his shooting at poor Meadowcroft, and leaving him for dead while he escaped with the money in the cart. He must have abandoned it at what he thought a convenient spot and made off with the cash, for nothing was found in the trap but the books and the hat."

"That seems the most curious part of all," I remarked. "For how came the hat in the cart when the wearer was found lying on the ground with no sign of any struggle?"

"You are certain there was no struggle?"

"Positive. Meadowcroft would have had extensive bruises or other evidence of the fact about him if there had been one. But have you traced the revolver?"

"Oh, that is very easily explained. A clerk going to the branch for the day and taking cash with him always carries one – more for the look of the thing, I admit, than anything else, for I never knew of one being used before. Whether Meadowcroft fired it in self-defence at the porter, or whether the porter fired it murderously at him, and, if so, how Meadowcroft ever let him get possession of it, I can't imagine."

"Then, after all, the revolver part of it seems a very simple affair." It was with almost a sense of disappointment that I heard this matter-of-fact explanation, and added, "I suppose you will be able to trace the notes?"

"Certainly. The numbers and all information were sent to the Bank of England and Scotland Yard the same evening. The cheques and papers in the bag would be, of course, quite valueless to Wells or anyone else. I would have staked my life on that man's honesty, but I suppose he gave way to a sudden temptation.

"Well, good evening. I hope if the patient remembers any more you will let me know. Perhaps, too, you wouldn't mind treating it with due secrecy."

I was about to make the natural protestation, when he added: "I mean that quite apart from your professional attitude, I hope you won't acquaint the police with anything fresh until we have an opportunity of talking it over together, as the bank doesn't care for too many details to be made public."

The next day was Saturday, and rather a busy one, so that I had no chance of speaking at length with Meadowcroft. He seemed on the whole to be a little more collected, but as he made no reference to the affair I was only too glad to avoid the subject. But it was fated that I should hear a great deal about it from other sources.

Returning from my morning rounds, I found Major awaiting me. His manner was portentous, and for reply to my query as to any fresh developments he silently handed me a shapeless lump of metal.

"Whatever is this?" I asked; and then, as I began to see in it a flattened mass of lead, "Is it the missing bullet?"

"That's it, sir. It took a little finding, but I spent nearly the whole of yesterday at the bank, for I knew that bullet must be somewhere about. Sure enough, after hunting round the back doorway for about an hour, I saw some fresh-looking splinters on the eaves a little to the right. So I got the ladder from the stable, and with a little more damage to the place, as you might say, I dug this here out of it."

"Good!" I exclaimed, and then with a recollection of the manager's caution, "How do you suppose it got there?"

"Well, I've been thinking that Mr Meadowcroft may have had his hand knocked up just as he was firing on Wells when he attacked him. Or it may have been the other way, and he may have knocked Wells' hand up as Wells was firing at him. It's a puzzle anyhow, and one we shan't get to the bottom of till one of them tells us. Has Mr Meadowcroft said anything about it?"

"Nothing fresh," I answered curtly.

"Well, it's one more step, this finding of the bullet, so I hope he'll say something soon, for there's but a poor chance of finding Wells, seemingly."

"He certainly has a good start."

"Ah, yes, doctor; but, you see, he's got the money."

Here Major's voice sank to a whisper, and he continued: "Bag found in the Loddon this morning – caught in some rushes – ripped open and quite empty."

"The same bag?"

"Stamped with the bank's name and all! Well, I must be getting on, sir. I just looked in on my way up to London. I've had a wire to go up to Scotland Yard about this case. Sorry you can't tell me more."

In the afternoon I had intended to have a talk with Meadowcroft, when a patient arrived, and then another and another, until I found the evening work was about to form a fitting close to a busy day. One of the women was especially garrulous and hard to dispose of, this affair having got on her nerves, as, indeed, it bid fair to get on mine. There was some excuse for her, however, as she was the wife of the new bank porter, Jackson, and complained of nervousness and insomnia.

She was sure the bank was haunted. Ghostly noises were to be heard at night near the scene of the tragedy. No one else heard them; her husband never heard anything – he would snore while she was being murdered. She seemed otherwise a sensible woman, and crediting her with a vivid imagination, I dismissed her with a mysterious tonic. I soon forgot her in the press of other work.

At length I was free, but then it was too late to talk with Meadowcroft. I postponed my interview until the next day, when, as will be seen, it was practically forced upon me.

I had arranged an easy morning's work, and returning about noon was told by the housekeeper that Meadowcroft was asking for me. I should observe that I had allowed him to read the newspaper the previous day, so that when I went upstairs the sight of a Sunday paper in his hand gave me no surprise. I had cause to regret my permission when he showed me a report of the case, which in detail extended to nearly a column.

An enterprising newspaper agency had even recorded the fact of the bullet being found. But there was a later and more startling item, to this effect:

We understand that the police have effected the arrest of a man alleged to be the bank porter Wells, who has been missing since the day of the occurrence. With a carelessness scarcely to be expected from his previous actions, the person who obtained possession of the cash which the unfortunate clerk was in charge of appears to have changed several notes for smaller sums in various places on the road between Reading and London, so that the police have been enabled to trace his progress with the greatest accuracy. A slight check was only to be expected when London was reached, had not a lucky accident enabled the police to arrest the alleged criminal. Early on Saturday morning, the proprietor of a lodging-house in the East India Dock Road gave information that a coloured seaman had been stabbed in a brawl with another inmate, who, on being taken into custody and searched, was found to have a large portion of the stolen property in his possession. When charged with the attempted murder and robbery at Ashtreecroft, the man, who gave the name of Stevens, stoutly protested his innocence, and declared he was able to establish a perfect alibi, and, although admitting that the property was not his own, made a statement as to having found it in a trap deserted by the roadside as he was on tramp from Reading.

Before I had read down the column I saw that any attempt to conceal matters from Meadowcroft might lead to unnecessary discussion, and probably excitement, which could only be injurious to him. So I sat down beside the sofa and calmly, and in as few words as possible, told him all that I knew.

I was relieved to find that he took it very quietly. Only occasionally did he interrupt me with questions, and their nature plainly showed that his memory was clarifying. Although I knew the counsel was rather impracticable, I endeavoured to persuade him not to let his thoughts dwell upon the matter. During the rest of the day, which I spent with him, I took every precaution to lead the conversation into other channels. When I got him off to bed at last I felt satisfied with my success.

The first visitor to the surgery on Monday was Jackson, the porter from the bank. It seemed that the noises which so alarmed his wife persisted. He was, he agreed with her, a sound sleeper, and had never heard them. But last night she had roused him in the small hours, and insisted on his searching the premises. Of course he found nothing; but as his wife was highly nervous, starting at the slightest noise and becoming quite hysterical, he hoped I would come and see her. I agreed somewhat contemptuously. I was just setting out when Major came in.

"Well, doctor," said he, "I had my journey to London for nothing."

"Indeed; I saw in the paper that the stolen property was found on a man arrested for stabbing someone."

"That's true enough, sir. He admits finding it in the trap, but he's put forward the best alibi possible concerning the bank business. He says he was on his way from Reading gaol when he met the trap about a mile away from there. And I called at the prison yesterday and found it was quite true. A man exactly answering to his description had been doing fourteen days, and for some insubordination was not discharged in the morning, but detained as punishment till four p.m."

"Then you are not much further forward?"

"Only as to recovering the money. It's all safe except about thirty pounds, which this man will have to answer for. But I've called, doctor, to ask you to let Mr Meadowcroft come round to the bank. Perhaps, if he has a look round, he may remember something which will help us."

I was privately rather inclined to this course myself, and as Meadowcroft at once fell in with the suggestion, we all went round together.

"Well," said Major to the clerk as we stood in the yard, "here you were found lying, and up above the door there I found the revolver bullet. Now, sir, can you remember who fired it?"

"Yes!" exclaimed Meadowcroft. "That newspaper report brought it all back to me yesterday. I seem to see it in a dream. I got into the trap with the bag, Wells handed me the reins, and I was driving off, when I remembered that I had laid down the revolver in the passage. Wells ran back for it, and I leant over and took it from him. The horse was restive, and attending more to him than to Wells, I caught the revolver awkwardly, and it went off as I held it."

"And then you fell?" I prompted him as he paused.

"Heaven knows!"

"Yes, but you did!" I insisted. "You were not wounded in any way. You were bruised exactly as you would have been by such a fall. The horse, as you tell us, was a restive brute, and of course it plunged about and perhaps kicked when the revolver went off, and so you were thrown out of the cart."

"But what became of Wells?" objected Major.

"Help! Help!" shrieked a woman's voice at this instant.

We all ran towards the door, just as the porter's wife rushed from it in a frenzy of terror.

"The ghost! The ghost!" she cried, and collapsed into Major's arms.

I heard a growl of something which sounded like "Keep quiet or I'll brain you!" and one of the most woe-begotten and forlorn objects I have ever seen rushed along the passage, then stopped, amazed at the sight of us, and leant gasping against the door-post. It was a man, haggard and filthy, his face covered with many days' stubble, who crouched blinking and shading his eyes with one hand, the other grasping a coal-hammer, his jaws inarticulately chattering the while.

"Why, if it isn't Wells!" roared Major.

On this the creature recovered his voice, and clawing at Meadowcroft as if fending off some horrid apparition, he huskily ejaculated:

"Take him away! It's not true – I never done it!"

"Why, Wells, don't you know me?" asked Meadowcroft, holding his hand out to him.

"Keep off! Don't come a-haunting me in daylight!" the man screamed, shuffling back into the passage.

By this time the fresh air had revived the porter's wife, so propping her against the step Major dashed after the retreating figure, who was stumbling towards a dark and narrow stairway. Dragging him back by the collar of his dilapidated coat, Major confronted him with Meadowcroft.

"It's all right, Wells. Don't be frightened," said the latter soothingly.

"Why, are – aren't you dead, sir?" stammered the poor wretch.

"Not a bit of it! Feel me!" and with that he grasped the dirty one's hand and wrung it, by no means gently.

"Oh, the Lord be praised! I thought you were shot!"

"Well, who did it?" asked Major.

"Not me – not me! It was an accident."

Meadowcroft and I exchanged glances.

"But tell us," I asked "how did it happen?"

"Oh, my! You're sure it's all right? I ain't a murderer, am I?" and he began to whimper, as much, I could see, from the effects of weakness as from the mental strain he must have gone through.

"Oh, Mr Meadowcroft, the pistol went off as I handed it to you, and the horse reared – I always said he was too flighty for our work – and you fell out of the cart, and I thought you were shot, and everyone would say I did it, and I should perish on the scaffold, and – and I didn't know what to do!"

"But what became of the horse and trap?" asked Meadowcroft.

"He galloped out of the yard, bad luck to him! And then I was sure they'd say I shot you to get the money. I ran downstairs to the furthest cellar, and there I hid. Oh, dear! Oh, dear! What I've suffered these five days down in that cellar with all the slugs and devil's coach-horses and horrid things. I never came out in daylight till today, and then I ran straight against this good lady, whoever she is, and she screamed so I thought the whole place would be aroused, and it would all be up with me."

"You haven't had much to eat?" I suggested.

"No, sir, indeed that's true. I used to try and forage a bit in the larder o' nights, but I feared to take much in case they'd miss it."

"Yes!" chimed in the lady indignantly, "frightening folks out of their senses wandering about all night! I thought the food was going faster than it ought, but I didn't say nothing, as I knew ghosts didn't eat, and my husband would only have laughed at me."

"Well, now that Wells has turned up at last, I wonder what ought to be done with him?" said Major, who seemed half-inclined to take the unfortunate porter into custody.

"Give him a wash and a good meal," said I.

It was quite six months later as we passed the bank on a market day that I asked my wife whether the substantial figure in a porter's uniform at the door quite realised her ideal of a ghost. But I regret to say that neither his "presence" nor the dignity of his office protected Wells from the ribaldry of the village boys, who, after the manner of their tribe, do not suffer him to forget his painful experience.

# R Austin Freeman

## The D'Arblay Mystery

When a man is found floating beneath the skin of a green-skimmed pond one morning, Dr Thorndyke becomes embroiled in an astonishing case. This wickedly entertaining detective fiction reveals that the victim was murdered through a lethal injection and someone out there is trying a cover-up.

## Dr Thorndyke Intervenes

What would you do if you opened a package to find a man's head? What would you do if the headless corpse had been swapped for a case of bullion? What would you do if you knew a brutal murderer was out there, somewhere, and waiting for you? Some people would run. Dr Thorndyke intervenes.

# R Austin Freeman

## Felo De Se

John Gillam was a gambler. John Gillam faced financial ruin and was the victim of a sinister blackmail attempt. John Gillam is now dead. In this exceptional mystery, Dr Thorndyke is brought in to untangle the secrecy surrounding the death of John Gillam, a man not known for insanity and thoughts of suicide.

## Flighty Phyllis

Chronicling the adventures and misadventures of Phyllis Dudley, Richard Austin Freeman brings to life a charming character always getting into scrapes. From impersonating a man to discovering mysterious trap doors, *Flighty Phyllis* is an entertaining glimpse at the times and trials of a wayward woman.

# R Austin Freeman

## Helen Vardon's Confession

Through the open door of a library, Helen Vardon hears an argument that changes her life forever. Helen's father and a man called Otway argue over missing funds in a trust one night. Otway proposes a marriage between him and Helen in exchange for his co-operation and silence. What transpires is a captivating tale of blackmail, fraud and death. Dr Thorndyke is left to piece together the clues in this enticing mystery.

## Mr Pottermack's Oversight

Mr Pottermack is a law-abiding, settled homebody who has nothing to hide until the appearance of the shadowy Lewison, a gambler and blackmailer with an incredible story. It appears that Pottermack is in fact a runaway prisoner, convicted of fraud, and Lewison is about to spill the beans unless he receives a large bribe in return for his silence. But Pottermack protests his innocence, and resolves to shut Lewison up once and for all. Will he do it? And if he does, will he get away with it?

## OTHER TITLES BY R AUSTIN FREEMAN AVAILABLE DIRECT FROM HOUSE OF STRATUS

| Quantity | | £ | $(US) | $(CAN) | € |
|---|---|---|---|---|---|
| | A CERTAIN DR THORNDYKE | 6.99 | 11.50 | 16.95 | 11.50 |
| | THE D'ARBLAY MYSTERY | 6.99 | 11.50 | 16.95 | 11.50 |
| | DR THORNDYKE INTERVENES | 6.99 | 11.50 | 16.95 | 11.50 |
| | DR THORNDYKE'S CASEBOOK | 6.99 | 11.50 | 16.95 | 11.50 |
| | THE EYE OF OSIRIS | 6.99 | 11.50 | 16.95 | 11.50 |
| | FELO DE SE | 6.99 | 11.50 | 16.95 | 11.50 |
| | FLIGHTY PHYLLIS | 6.99 | 11.50 | 16.95 | 11.50 |
| | THE GOLDEN POOL: A STORY OF A FORGOTTEN MINE | 6.99 | 11.50 | 16.95 | 11.50 |
| | THE GREAT PORTRAIT MYSTERY | 6.99 | 11.50 | 16.95 | 11.50 |
| | HELEN VARDON'S CONFESSION | 6.99 | 11.50 | 16.95 | 11.50 |

ALL HOUSE OF STRATUS BOOKS ARE AVAILABLE FROM GOOD BOOKSHOPS OR DIRECT FROM THE PUBLISHER:

Internet: **www.houseofstratus.com** including author interviews, reviews, features.

Email: **sales@houseofstratus.com** please quote author, title and credit card details.

# OTHER TITLES BY R AUSTIN FREEMAN AVAILABLE DIRECT
## FROM HOUSE OF STRATUS

| Quantity | £ | $(US) | $(CAN) | € |
|---|---|---|---|---|
| Mr Polton Explains | 6.99 | 11.50 | 16.95 | 11.50 |
| Mr Pottermack's Oversight | 6.99 | 11.50 | 16.95 | 11.50 |
| The Mystery of 31 New Inn | 6.99 | 11.50 | 16.95 | 11.50 |
| The Mystery of Angelina Frood | 6.99 | 11.50 | 16.95 | 11.50 |
| The Penrose Mystery | 6.99 | 11.50 | 16.95 | 11.50 |
| The Puzzle Lock | 6.99 | 11.50 | 16.95 | 11.50 |
| The Red Thumb Mark | 6.99 | 11.50 | 16.95 | 11.50 |
| The Shadow of the Wolf | 6.99 | 11.50 | 16.95 | 11.50 |
| A Silent Witness | 6.99 | 11.50 | 16.95 | 11.50 |
| The Singing Bone | 6.99 | 11.50 | 16.95 | 11.50 |

ALL HOUSE OF STRATUS BOOKS ARE AVAILABLE FROM GOOD BOOKSHOPS
OR DIRECT FROM THE PUBLISHER:

**Hotline:** UK ONLY: 0800 169 1780, please quote author, title and credit card details.
INTERNATIONAL: +44 (0) 20 7494 6400, please quote author, title, and credit card details.

**Send to:** House of Stratus Sales Department
24c Old Burlington Street
London
W1X 1RL
UK

Please allow for postage costs charged per order plus an amount per book as set out in the tables below:

| | £(Sterling) | $(US) | $(CAN) | €(Euros) |
|---|---|---|---|---|
| **Cost per order** | | | | |
| UK | 2.00 | 3.00 | 4.50 | 3.30 |
| Europe | 3.00 | 4.50 | 6.75 | 5.00 |
| North America | 3.00 | 4.50 | 6.75 | 5.00 |
| Rest of World | 3.00 | 4.50 | 6.75 | 5.00 |
| **Additional cost per book** | | | | |
| UK | 0.50 | 0.75 | 1.15 | 0.85 |
| Europe | 1.00 | 1.50 | 2.30 | 1.70 |
| North America | 2.00 | 3.00 | 4.60 | 3.40 |
| Rest of World | 2.50 | 3.75 | 5.75 | 4.25 |

PLEASE SEND CHEQUE, POSTAL ORDER (STERLING ONLY), EUROCHEQUE, OR INTERNATIONAL MONEY ORDER (PLEASE CIRCLE METHOD OF PAYMENT YOU WISH TO USE)
MAKE PAYABLE TO: STRATUS HOLDINGS plc

Cost of book(s): —————————— Example: 3 x books at £6.99 each: £20.97

Cost of order: —————————— Example: £2.00 (Delivery to UK address)

Additional cost per book: —————— Example: 3 x £0.50: £1.50

Order total including postage: ———— Example: £24.47

Please tick currency you wish to use and add total amount of order:

☐ £ (Sterling)    ☐ $ (US)    ☐ $ (CAN)    ☐ € (EUROS)

VISA, MASTERCARD, SWITCH, AMEX, SOLO, JCB:

☐ ☐ ☐ ☐ ☐ ☐ ☐ ☐ ☐ ☐ ☐ ☐ ☐ ☐ ☐ ☐ ☐ ☐

**Issue number (Switch only):**

☐ ☐ ☐

**Start Date:**                    **Expiry Date:**

☐☐ / ☐☐                         ☐☐ / ☐☐

Signature: ————————————

NAME: ————————————————————

ADDRESS: ——————————————————

————————————————————

POSTCODE: ——————

Please allow 28 days for delivery.

Prices subject to change without notice.
Please tick box if you do not wish to receive any additional information. ☐

House of Stratus publishes many other titles in this genre; please check our website (**www.houseofstratus.com**) for more details.